BEYOND ALL REASON

BY PEGGY J. HERRING

D0109957

Bella
BOOKS

Ferndale, Michigan
2002

Bella Books, Inc.
P.O. Box 201007
Ferndale, MI 48220

Printed in the United States of America on acid-free paper
First Edition

Editor: Greg Herren
Cover designer: Bonnie Liss (Phoenix Graphics)

ISBN 1-931513-25-2

For Polly Hawkey

*We've known each other
for a LONG TIME
and I'll remember your bravery forever.*

Acknowledgments

I would like to thank Frankie J. Jones for being my first reader and for her insight into how to make a story better.

I would also like to thank Dr. Sean T. O'Mara, M.D. for his input into the medical aspects of this novel.

Laurie McMillen — thanks for your constant support and encouragement. You helped bring a touch of realism to the story with your own area of expertise. Your help was truly appreciated.

Helen V. Gallagher — thanks for tapping that ruler and reminding me about the deadline.

'Zann — your vast knowledge of the hotel industry was invaluable to me. I appreciate your willingness to share it and to elaborate on your entertaining experiences as only you can do.

A very special thanks goes to Polly Hawkey for her honesty, courage and enthusiasm for brainstorming. I'm looking forward to more of the same.

Beyond All Reason is based on a short story titled "Always A Bridesmaid" that first appeared in the Naiad Anthology *The First Time Ever*.

PART I

TRINA

Spring

Chapter One

Trina set her suitcase down and smiled tiredly at the desk clerk. She told the young man her name, wanting to just go to her room and get into something more comfortable.

"How are things in Dallas, Ms. LaRue?" the desk clerk asked. According to his name tag, his name was Joseph. He was about Trina's height, which was average for a man. He parted his dark shoulder-length hair in the middle, making him look younger than he probably was. She liked the fact that he knew her already and why she was there.

Trina smiled again. Being an employee of the Regal Palace Hotel chain gave her less privacy than a regular guest, but she didn't mind since her accommodations were free. It was just one of many perks the Palace gave its employees.

"Dallas is Dallas," she said. "It's basically all the same."

They exchanged a look that relayed a mutual understanding. Employees of the Regal Palace Hotel system learned early in their careers to never openly discuss the shortcomings of the company they worked for.

"Room 3332," Joseph said as he handed her the small rectangle-shaped envelope that held her plastic key card. "Interviews will be in the Crockett Room down this hallway."

"Thank you."

"Good luck and enjoy your stay. The elevators are down the other hall and to the left."

She picked up her suitcase and purse and felt better. It had been a long day. Trina had already put in ten hours of work before catching the flight from Dallas to San Antonio. She was still mulling over her employment options and had a few concerns about applying for a new position.

Born and raised in San Antonio, it surprised her how unsettled she felt each time she came back. She only had a few good memories here and thought of each visit as some sort of punishment she needed to endure. But Rosalie and Trina's Aunt Reba lived in San Antonio. They were the only reasons she would ever consider trying to make this place her home again. San Antonio was the ninth largest city in the United States. There had to be a way to live in a town that big and not bump into her parents everywhere she went.

Trina stepped off the elevator and easily found room 3332. She stuck the key card into the slot until the light on the door blinked green. She turned the handle and opened the door, but didn't notice right away the rumpled sheets or the two naked bodies going at it on the bed. The woman saw her first and screamed. The man on top of her was too involved in his search for pleasure to care what was going on. The woman finally bucked him off and hastily covered herself with a sheet. Only then did the man realize they were not alone. He scrambled up and covered himself with both hands, although one hand would have been quite sufficient.

4

Trina managed to mumble an apology before leaving the room, luggage in tow. She stormed toward the elevator. Once back in the lobby again, she headed straight for the front desk.

"How can I help you, Ms. LaRue?" Joseph asked pleasantly.

"I'd prefer to have my *own* room," she said and set the envelope containing the key card on the counter. "There was already someone in 3332." Trina made an effort to keep her irritation under control.

"I'm terribly sorry!" Joseph's eyes were huge.

And they were naked! she wanted to snap. *Naked, naked, naked!* But she continued to keep her temper in check. There was a chance she would have to work with these people in the future, so taking her frustration out on whoever was working at the front desk now wouldn't be wise.

"There's been a mistake," Joseph said.

Trina gave him her best "no kidding" look.

"I don't see how this could have happened. Hmm. Someone gave her your room. I'm very sorry. I just came on duty about an hour ago." He scribbled something down and took the key card she had put on the counter. "I can give you Room 3334."

"I don't want to be anywhere near those people! Put me on another floor."

"Yes, ma'am. Not a problem."

The first thing Trina did when she opened the door to her new room was glance at the bed and make sure it was empty. After a quick visual inspection, she took off her shoes and began to unpack, taking special care to hang up the blue suit she had brought to wear for her interview the next morning. As she lined up her toiletries in the bathroom, she forced herself not to wonder what was going on in room 3332 right

5

then. *Nothing quite like getting caught in the act to kill a mood,* she thought with a chuckle.

Trina began thinking about the job she was applying for. She was qualified for the position. Her résumé spoke for itself, so she wasn't concerned about that. She felt certain this job was hers if she wanted it. That, however, was the big question she had to find the answer to fairly soon. Did she really want it?

Trina switched on the television, changed into shorts and a T-shirt, putting off the phone call to Rosalie a few minutes longer. In an effort to shake the uneasiness she was continuing to feel, Trina stretched out on the bed and did some channel surfing first. As she pushed the button on the remote she cleared her mind and tried to relax. Trina liked hotel rooms and their predictability. Staying in a hotel never failed to make her appreciate her apartment once she returned from a trip. It was nice to get away and be pampered occasionally.

She stopped on one of the movie channels. There was a scene showing a horse-drawn sleigh being pulled through the snow. It reminded her of what she thought Christmas should really be like. A south Texas Christmas usually involved the possibility of rain, a light jacket, and houses decorated with glowing nativity scenes and wooden reindeer stuck on a lawn. As Trina stacked pillows under her head, she thought about the last several Christmases she had spent with her Aunt Reba. Christmas was also the only time of year she saw her parents and her brother Arty. Trina always took extra time finding nice gifts for them, and spared no expense in buying things she knew they would like. This past Christmas had been especially interesting with Rosalie there.

Rosalie, she thought with a sigh. *What a wonderful, passionate woman she is.*

At the time Trina and Rosalie met, Rosalie was engaged to Trina's brother Arty. Even though Trina had been estranged from her immediate family for well over ten years, she still made her annual trip to see them on Christmas Day despite how her parents and her brother felt about her. Reminding them she was still a part of the family was just one of several reasons she went to see them every year. She had never regretted telling her parents she was a lesbian when she was seventeen. In return, her parents had never regretted throwing her out of their house immediately afterward.

With the clothes on her back and less than four dollars in her pocket, Trina had found a pay phone that dreadful March night and called her Aunt Reba. Twenty minutes later, Aunt Reba and her house mate, Juanito Gomez, came to pick her up at a convenience store. Trina lived with them until she graduated from high school fifteen months later. Neither her parents nor her brother ever called to see where she was or how she was doing. It was as if she had ceased to exist for them all together.

Aunt Reba had also been an outcast from the family for many years. She was a lesbian as well and shared her home with Juanito, an older gay man. It seemed natural for Trina to live with them. Aunt Reba made sure Trina felt loved and wanted. In return, Trina had done her best to stay out of trouble and go on with her life. Aunt Reba's own sexual preference had never been openly discussed in front of Trina, but she had heard the rumors and innuendoes from her family most of her life. Trina felt safe and somewhat at peace living with Aunt Reba and Juanito, never looking back after her parents had disowned her. Trina set out to make something of herself, despite what her parents thought of her, but her estrangement from them still troubled her.

It was only natural that she still had some difficulty struggling with the fact the LaRues had so much power over her. She was confused about how they had taken it upon themselves to sever the ties without even giving her a chance to either agree or disagree with such a decision. But even though they had made it very clear they wanted nothing to do with a lesbian daughter, Trina returned for a visit once a year on Christmas Day. She would enter their home bearing wonderful gifts to place under the Christmas tree. She would ask her parents and her brother how they were, and comment briefly on their appearance. Trina would glance around the house, and notice that it was exactly the same way she remembered it as a child at Christmas: the same white twinkling lights outlining the house's shape on the outside . . . the garland on the mantel over the fireplace . . . the angel on top of the tree with the faded brown belly where the bulb inside had scorched it. Then there was the smell of a turkey roasting in the oven, and ripe oranges in the huge green bowl of fruit on the coffee table. Both of those scents woke up her sensory perception when she arrived. The turkey and the oranges still had such an amazing affect on her, that whenever she encountered either of those smells anywhere else they both immediately made her think of past Christmases with her family.

But those were the good memories of life with the LaRues, and had little to do with the new traditions Trina and her family had started during the holidays. Trina became a different person for about ten minutes out of the year when she took the time to see her parents on Christmas Day. Trina was a stranger to her emotions during that time, but it didn't stop her from carrying on and being just as childish as her brother and her parents were. Something else took over then . . . something in her head and her heart. That "something" always made Trina do the same thing over and over again. She would take the three beautifully wrapped presents she had bought and pull them out of the shopping bag. She would then place the gifts carefully under the LaRues' Christmas tree. After that Trina would move out of the way so her father, mother and brother could find which one belonged to them. Once that happened, Trina would watch as they each picked up their present before marching to the front door, opening it up and throwing their individual gift out on the lawn.

Thinking about this will only depress you, she reminded herself. Trina began flipping through the channels again until

8

she found a cooking program. The woman sautéing mush-rooms and onions reminded her of Rosalie. Once again, Trina wondered if interviewing for this new job was a good idea.

Trina had first heard about Rosalie from her Aunt Reba. The news about Arty's engagement to the beautiful elementary school teacher had spread through the LaRue family quickly, thanks to one in-law named Missy LaRue. Aunt Missy was married to Trina's Uncle Frederick, her father's brother. Aunt Missy loved to talk and never failed to keep Aunt Reba posted on what was going on. Trina and Aunt Reba spoke on the phone several times during the course of a week, so Trina was kept up-to-date on the gossip about the family and mutual friends via Reba's various chats with Aunt Missy. Most of the LaRues viewed Missy as nothing more than a busy-body with nothing better to do than gossip. Trina and Aunt Reba considered her a valuable source of information on what individual families in the LaRue clan were up to.

"I hear she's a very nice young woman," Aunt Reba had said one evening in late November, referring to Rosalie. "But I'm not sure what's wrong with her if she's planning to marry your brother."

"My thoughts exactly," Trina said. They both howled with laughter. "Maybe she needs some free plumbing or some-thing." The LaRue & Son Plumbing Company was a well-established and profitable business. Arty was known to get a lot of his dates from customers — single women with leaky faucets.

So Trina was aware her brother had a fiancée named Rosalie, and Rosalie would be there on Christmas Day when Trina made her annual visit. All Trina knew about her was she taught second grade and probably had self-esteem issues if she found someone like Arty LaRue suitable for marriage. Arty had his good looks going for him, but he was getting close

9

to thirty and still lived at home with his parents. The family home was paid for so there couldn't be many household expenses. Their mother cooked, cleaned and did Arty's laundry for him. He had it made. Trina also knew someday Arty would inherit the house once their parents died, so living there already would even save him from having to move.

Living at home with his parents had to make being alone with his girlfriends an interesting challenge for Arty. Any time they spent alone would undoubtedly involve sleeping over at his girlfriend's place. From what Trina remembered about her brother, he was too cheap to spring for a hotel each time he and his girlfriend wanted to be together.

Trina also found herself being curious about the type of woman who would be attracted to her brother. What she discovered when she met Rosalie Cofax, however, changed her life forever.

Chapter Two

Trina continued to channel surf and gradually began to relax. She and Rosalie would probably order from room service later. Trina liked thinking about Rosalie, and how they had gotten to know each other after that short Christmas Day meeting just three months ago.

She reached for the phone and dialed Rosalie's number. Each and every time Trina called her, she half expected to get a message on Rosalie's answering machine. As the telephone rang, Trina unconsciously acknowledged the possibility that Rosalie could be out with Arty. Trina knew how silly and irrational that line of thinking was, but she couldn't help herself. The only thing that seemed to bring her back from such feelings of jealousy and despair was the excitement she would hear in Rosalie's voice once she realized who was calling her. *You can't fake that kind of enthusiasm*, Trina often reminded herself, but even after three months of making love, exchanging email and late-night phone calls, Trina couldn't get over the fact that Rosalie had at one time been Arty's fiancée.

Trina had definite trust issues, and had even considered going back into therapy over this Rosalie-Arty thing. Her inability to trust anyone had begun the night her parents had disowned her. In her mind, if her own parents couldn't love her, then no one else probably could either. She had a string of ex-lovers who told her more than once she needed to learn how to open up and give something back. Trina couldn't bring herself to take most women too seriously when it came to love and affairs of the heart. The closer they wanted to get to her, the harder she would push them away. Dating straight women had been the answer for a short period of time. She enjoyed their charm and curiosity, but those relationships had also gone sour because of her own inability and unwillingness to trust a lover.

"Hello?"

"Hi," Trina said, nervously clutching the phone. "It's me."

"Hi, baby!"

Trina smiled at the delight in Rosalie's voice.

"Where are you? I didn't recognize the number on my Caller ID."

"I'm at the Regal Palace River Walk. The one across from River Center."

"You're here in San Antonio? Really?"

"I have a business meeting in the morning."

"What's your room number? I can be there in twenty minutes."

Trina received another call from her once Rosalie was in her car. Rosalie was obviously excited about her unexpected visit; she was chatty and carried most of the conversation. It still amazed Trina that whenever they were together, they never discussed Arty. Trina was still trying to understand what Rosalie had seen in him in the first place. This unnerving interest Trina had in her brother and his ex-girlfriend was getting in the way of any peace of mind Trina hoped to have where this new relationship was concerned. Getting past who Rosalie had chosen to be with at one time wasn't proving to be easy; Trina wasn't sure she would ever be able to come to terms with the fact that Arty and Rosalie had once been lovers. Trust was such a fragile thing. Trina understood that she lacked the courage to get over the fact that Rosalie had been with someone like Arty — someone with Rush Limbaugh bumper stickers on his truck and who thought the decline of humanity rested solely on the shoulders of all feminists.

Trina often thought of her brother as a simple guy of slow wit. He was also fortunate in the fact he had a permanent job in the family-owned business he would someday inherit. All of Arty's friends were just like him. They met for bowling on Wednesday nights, played softball on Saturday evenings nine months out of the year and had the sports channel on all day on Sunday. Arty spent most of his spare time with his friends and their women. He didn't smoke, but enjoyed an occasional beer. Like his father, he worked hard and spoke harshly about women who took well-paying jobs that should be held by men. Also like his father, Arty disliked the Japanese, Koreans, Chinese and Russians. On several occasions, he made it known he detested gays and would be horrified if word ever got out again that his sister was a lesbian. Trina wondered if Arty ever had an original thought. He had been groomed on prejudice acquired from their father. He and Trina had both been exposed to it their whole lives. Arty had taken it to heart, while Trina had rebelled against the name calling and stereotyping at an early age.

With a high school education, a few years at a trade school and a plumbing license to his credit, Arty was good with people. He had a boyish charm that kept him supplied with girlfriends most of the time. Life had been good to Arty LaRue, and Trina was embarrassed to admit she resented everything that seemed to have come his way. As children they had gotten along fine. They spent a lot of time playing with Arty's toys and enjoyed throwing a baseball or football to each other or engaging in a cowboy shoot-out with other kids in the neighborhood. If teams for games were chosen, Arty made sure his little sister was always on his side, ensuring a win. But everything changed once they both got to high school. As girls became increasingly more important to both of them, their relationship gradually began to deteriorate.

Trina checked in the mirror and ran her fingers through her hair. *What will you do if you get this job you're interviewing for tomorrow,* she wondered. *Aunt Reba would like having you closer, but this town might be way too small for you and the LaRues.* Trina had to give it more serious thought between now and tomorrow morning. The job itself would not be a problem; that she was certain of. But living in a city like San Antonio again would almost be like having one foot back in the closet. Unlike Austin, Houston or Dallas, in San Antonio gays and lesbians had no real place to call their own other than a few bars that were constantly closing. Trina wasn't a bar person. Part of her job involved managing a hotel lounge for a living, so she saw no need to go to bars just because lesbians might be there. San Antonio had a huge gay and lesbian population because of the four military installations located there, but not a lot of people were out. As a result, there were few gay-owned businesses. A trip to Austin was in order just to find a rainbow sticker anywhere. Giving up an established gay and lesbian community, like the one she now had in Dallas, would also carry some weight in her decision about whether or not to take the job. She liked the openness, the diversity and the safety of being around gay people in general. She knew where to go to find them in Dallas. Friends and a sense of community weren't everything, though. Compared to being with Aunt Reba and Rosalie again, friends and a community were small considerations when it came to her final decision to move.

Trina didn't get nervous until she heard the knock on her door. Rosalie came in with a small suitcase, clearly intending to spend the night. She set the suitcase down, put her arms around Trina's neck and kissed her deeply.

For Trina, Rosalie's passion was nothing short of amazing each time she experienced it. Trina always remembered her as being warm, cuddly and delicious, but the intensity of Rosalie's desire never failed to rock Trina's very foundation. Her kisses were hot and possessive, with Rosalie taking Trina's head in her hands and toying with her hair while their lips continued saying hello. Rosalie then took Trina in her arms and hugged her tightly.

"It's so good to hold you again," she whispered. "What a nice surprise having you here."

"I'm glad you could make it." Trina kissed her neck, almost swooning at the sweet scent of her hair and perfume. *Sure you're coming back here for Aunt Reba*, she thought with a shake of her head.

Trina took her by the hand and led her to the bed. They sat down on the edge and looked at each other for a moment. Rosalie couldn't keep her hands to herself and began touching Trina's neck and playing with her hair again. They fell back on the bed and slowly began to kiss. Trina wanted to keep her there this way forever.

No words were spoken, only a series of small moans and sighs. As the slow kisses continued, Trina could feel Rosalie's desire almost radiating from her body. Each time they got to this point — the physical closeness and heated foreplay — Trina realized how silly it was to ever worry about the likes of Arty LaRue.

"I've missed you so much," Rosalie said as she reached over and rubbed Trina's breast through her T-shirt.

Trina closed her eyes and sighed before kissing her again. Being touched by Rosalie left her feeling dizzy from pleasure. Trina was the one with all the experience, but Rosalie's uncanny ability to know when and where to touch her invariably managed to catch Trina off guard. Being Rosalie's first lesbian lover, Trina never expected such confidence in someone so new to lesbian lovemaking. Rosalie had been an avid student from the beginning and was very good at what she did.

They continued to kiss. Trina liked knowing Rosalie enjoyed kissing just as much as she did. After a while, they moved on to touching each other through their clothes, and then, eventually removing various articles of clothing as things progressed. There was no focused attempt at prolonging their foreplay. It came naturally to them and was as much fun as bringing each other to orgasm. Trina firmly believed that only a woman knew how to kiss another woman, and she understood how important it was to a partner that her lover be good at it. Rosalie seemed to excel at this as well as other things. She had a talent for getting Trina so hot it seemed as though her clothes would disintegrate from her smoldering body. Slow, deep kissing could do that for her. Trina was no longer surprised by the effect this woman had on her.

"You smell so nice," Rosalie whispered, nuzzling Trina's neck and sucking an earlobe into her mouth. Trina trembled as a delightful ripple of pleasure traveled through her body. Rosalie's hand returned to Trina's breast and brushed against her nipple. Trina was on fire and searched for Rosalie's lips again.

After a moment, Rosalie broke away from the kiss and covered Trina's breast with her mouth through the T-shirt. She kissed her again as they both struggled to lift up Trina's shirt. Rosalie wasted no time taking Trina's bare breast into her mouth and then sucking and flicking her tongue over the hard nipple. She left one breast and then did the same to the other. Rosalie seemed to be lost in her actions, truly enjoying what she was doing.

More kissing followed as they both slipped off their shirts, but now touching became equally as important. Trina loved Rosalie's firm, perky breasts and the way she squirmed when Trina circled one nipple with her tongue and the other nipple with a wet fingertip. Finally taking one into her mouth and tugging gently made the most incredible sigh come from deep inside Rosalie's throat.

"Harder, baby," Rosalie whispered breathlessly.

Trina loved it when Rosalie called her baby. She gladly sucked harder and then helped find a better position, taking full advantage of the huge bed and the fact Rosalie wanted her mouth on Trina's breast at the same time. The ability to concentrate on pleasing her lover was a challenge for Trina the moment Rosalie began licking her nipples and creating a feast of her own. When they were both ready for more, their lips found each other again and hot, deep kissing suddenly became the emergency. They broke away from each other long enough to get out of the rest of their clothes. Rosalie reached for her and pulled Trina closer as their hot, naked bodies touched for the first time since Rosalie's arrival. They began kissing again. Their hands were everywhere, running up and down bare thighs and arms. Trina was ready to come, so she rolled Rosalie over on her back and began nibbling and kissing her way down Rosalie's body, beginning at her breasts and slowly along her soft, warm belly. As Trina inched her way downward, she licked and nipped Rosalie's sweet, pale flesh. She positioned herself between Rosalie's open legs, loving the womanly scent of her desire.

Trina nuzzled the light thatch of hair and smiled at the dampness she found there. She kissed the inside of each thigh and then spread Rosalie open with her fingers. Reintroducing herself to her lover, Trina touched the tip of her tongue to the very center of her. Rosalie sighed, "Oh, baby . . ."

Trina flattened her tongue and licked her slowly. Rosalie opened her legs farther and reached down to lace her fingers through Trina's hair.

"Oh, baby . . ." Rosalie said again. "That feels so good . . . so good."

Trina knew they would both want this again soon and Rosalie would come harder the second time she tasted her. She searched for the center of her and gently sucked until rewarded with Rosalie's hands on the back of her head. Then, soon afterward, that was accompanied by a slow undulation of hips gradually increasing into a definite bucking motion as they both rode an incredible wave of heat and passion. The hands on the back of Trina's head were what made her personally wet, aching for more. From the few times they had been together, Trina had discovered Rosalie liked direct stimulation the first time, and then slow and sweet probing the second.

Afterward, Rosalie was weak and mellow. "Oh, baby," she said again. "Come here." She tugged on Trina's ear. "Come here and let me hold you for a minute."

Trina kissed the inside of Rosalie's thighs again, and wiped the wetness from her face onto her T-shirt. Once Trina was in her arms, Rosalie smiled and kissed her nose.

"Your turn, lover," she said, then let her tongue trace along the side of Trina's breast.

"I'm on the verge of a meltdown," Trina said huskily. "Just touch me. That's all I'll need."

"Oh, you're no fun," Rosalie said with a sleepy grin. As she continued to concentrate on Trina's breasts, her hand rubbed across her soft belly, slowly moving down to Trina's thigh. Rosalie's hand then came back up, and gently mingled in her damp triangle. "A meltdown?" she said, and touched Trina's nipple with her tongue at the same time that she slid her fingers into delightfully moist folds. Trina was indeed wet and throbbing.

"Ohhh," Trina said as she began to move her hips. She

covered Rosalie's hand with her own to intensify the pressure and deepen the penetration. Trina came quickly, and thought she would pass out from such a powerful sensation. When it was over, she was cuddly and loved the way Rosalie kept her fingers inside of her as they held each other. They fell asleep that way, and woke up an hour later to start all over again.

Chapter Three

Trina glanced at the clock the next morning when she heard the phone ring for their wake-up call. She got up and went to the bathroom. Rosalie was napping against the wall outside the bathroom door when she came out.

"You look so cute all sleepy and naked," Trina said, giving her a quick hug and a pat on the butt as Rosalie sleepily trudged past her.

"How much time do we have?" Rosalie asked when she came back to bed.

Trina grinned. "My appointment is at eight, so I have two and a half hours. You have to get a shower, drive across town in early morning traffic and be at school by 7:30, so I'd say you have about forty-five minutes."

Rosalie laughed and gave her a playful swat on the arm.

Trina propped herself up on an elbow and looked down at her. Rosalie's blond hair was scrambled from sleep, but fanned out across the pillow and looked great. The sight of her tugged at Trina's heart.

"You want to sleep longer?" Trina asked. She gently ran a finger along Rosalie's bare arm.

With her eyes closed, Rosalie told her how she liked being sweetly coaxed awake.

"I see," Trina said. She replaced her finger with her lips and began kissing along Rosalie's arm. "Like this, maybe?" She saw Rosalie smile.

"Yes, something like that."

Rosalie pulled her down and kissed her. Trina rolled on top of her and felt a very nice connection as Rosalie worked her leg in between Trina's. Amazed at how quickly Rosalie could make her so wet and hot, Trina realized Rosalie was also ready.

"This is how I want to wake up every morning," Rosalie whispered.

Trina was concentrating on how good she was feeling, and how much better she was about to feel. Rosalie captured a swaying breast with both hands and sucked on the nipple as though her life depended on it. That was exactly the stimulation Trina had needed in order to come, and she began moving against Rosalie as they linked their bodies together in urgency.

"God, I love this," Rosalie said as they moved with a more definite purpose.

All the elements were in place for Trina and she could feel the physical equivalent to an explosion on its way. In Trina's mind Rosalie's instincts about how to make it better for her . . . for them both . . . were uncanny. Trina felt wild with sensation as they continued to rub against each other until they were both so hot nothing could stop what was happening. Rosalie grabbed Trina's hips and desperately pulled her closer.

They were both at the mercy of orgasmic bliss. Trina could hear her own low, husky moans mixed in with Rosalie's right after they came together. Rosalie had her hands on Trina's back and pulled her even closer as she raised her own hips to meet her.

Once their shuddering finally stopped and they both began to tremble with exertion, they hugged and held onto each other until a wonderful throbbing afterglow allowed them to be still and bask in what had just happened.

Trina heard Rosalie sniff just before she hugged her again. Rosalie was laying in Trina's arms when a cool tear fell on Trina's chest. Trina moved blond hair away from Rosalie's forehead and kissed her there.

"Nothing like that has ever happened to me before," Rosalie said, her voice thick with emotion.

"I know," Trina whispered as she kissed her forehead again. "That was a first for me, too."

Trina had on her favorite dark blue powersuit, a light blue silk blouse, and dark blue matching heels. She checked her briefcase one more time to make sure her résumé and three letters of recommendation were with her. She had already sent copies of everything to Roscoe Hobart, the hotel's General Manager, but didn't want to take a chance on having her paperwork get lost. She had made up her mind to take the job if it was offered. She wanted to be closer to Rosalie.

Trina left her room, getting to the lobby almost ten minutes before her appointment. One of the clerks at the front desk, a young black woman with a pleasant smile, offered to check for her and make sure everything was on schedule. If Trina had to wait too long, there was a slim chance she'd get nervous. She didn't want that to happen.

"There's the other applicant now," the desk clerk said. "You should be next, Ms. LaRue."

As the other applicant walked by, Trina looked up and met the eyes of the woman she had caught in bed the previous afternoon after being assigned the wrong room. The woman turned a nice shade of red. Trina smiled and attempted to put her at ease.

"Trina LaRue from Dallas," she said and offered her hand to the woman. The woman's handshake was a limp squeeze in return. *Like shaking hands with a dead fish,* Trina thought.

The woman didn't offer her name. Her embarrassment was still quite visible. She appeared to be in her mid to late thirties. *She looks a lot younger when she's naked,* Trina mused.

"Any idea how many of us are being interviewed?" Trina asked.

"Uh . . . five, I believe. Will you excuse me? I need to check out and get to the airport. Apparently they won't make a decision until tomorrow." She walked away with more composure and self-confidence than Trina imagined she herself would have had under the circumstances.

"Who is she?" Trina asked the clerk.

"Mel Cambridge. F and B Manager from Houston."

So that's Mel Cambridge, Trina thought. She had heard the name a few times during the last six months, but had never met her. She and Trina held similar management positions in the Regal Palace Hotel chain, but Mel had only been promoted to management within the last year or so.

"Mr. Hobart's assistant should be out here shortly looking for you," the desk clerk said. "Ah . . . here she is now."

Trina turned around and saw a cute woman about her own age. She had red hair shaped in what could only be described as a Beatle cut. She was short and had the body of an athlete. *Softball,* Trina thought immediately. *I bet she plays softball.*

"You must be Trina LaRue," the woman said. "I'm Dee Cockran. Mr. Hobart's assistant. We spoke on the phone."

"Yes," Trina said and shook her hand, this time receiving a real handshake in return. "Nice to meet you. Are we ready?"

"Indeed we are," Dee said. "This way, please."

Trina followed her to a conference room named after Davy Crockett. That was the running theme of most hotels in the downtown San Antonio area. Crockett, Travis and Bowie were names of streets, elementary schools and parks throughout the city. Naturally, a conference room less than two blocks from the Alamo would honor these heroes.

Coffee, juice and pastries were on a cart just inside the door. A huge table surrounded by executive chairs took up a large part of the room. As Trina expected, the room was spotless, reflecting definite masculine qualities with dark blue carpet and brown trim around the windows and baseboards.

"Please help yourself to some refreshments," Dee said. "Mr. Hobart should be here shortly." Dee poured herself a cup of coffee and selected a blueberry muffin.

The door opened and Mr. Hobart came in. He and Trina saw each other at the same time and both immediately let out little gasps of surprise. Roscoe Hobart was the man Trina had seen naked the day before. He was the man who had been copulating like a six foot rabbit on top of Mel Cambridge in room 3332! *Mel Cambridge*, Trina thought suddenly. *One of the other applicants!* He at least had the decency to turn as red as Mel had a few minutes earlier.

Trina shrugged, disappointed. She had worked hard at convincing herself she had wanted this job.

"This will obviously be a total waste of my time," she heard herself saying.

Mr. Hobart opened the door. "Dee, I'll handle this one on my own. Thanks."

With a puzzled expression, Dee nodded and left with her coffee and muffin.

"Please have a seat, Ms. LaRue."

He's already made up his mind, she thought. *Mel Cambridge has the damn job I want!* Trina no longer cared

24

about being there. She just wanted to leave so she could think about what had happened and maybe have a nice little chuckle on the plane ride back to Dallas. It had been an interesting idea . . . living in San Antonio again and seeing more of Rosalie and Aunt Reba.

"This is quite embarrassing," Mr. Hobart finally said.

No kidding, Trina thought. Roscoe Hobart and his wife Nelda were General Managers at different hotels in town. Nelda Hobart managed the Regal Palace Hotel River Center across the street from this one and was known to run a tight ship. From what Trina could remember hearing, the Hobarts were described as fair and loyal to the company. Apparently, Roscoe wasn't all that fair and loyal to his wife.

"I've read your letters of recommendation and I'm impressed with your résumé, Ms. LaRue," he said as they sat down across from each other at the table. He kept his eyes on the papers in front of him, but occasionally made an effort to look at her. The situation was beyond awkward. Trina didn't know what to do. *How do I get myself into these situations,* she wondered. *How many other women in the world have accidentally walked in on their future boss while he's having sex?*

"Your degrees in Hotel Management and Business Management set your application apart from the others," he continued. "I've also heard good things about the work you're doing in Dallas. May I ask why you're interested in this position?"

"I have family and friends here in San Antonio," she said. *Rosalie,* she thought. *I could see Rosalie whenever I wanted to.* Trina began to relax a little. She might actually get a fair interview despite the circumstances. For the first time since she recognized him as "the naked guy in room 3332," Trina allowed herself to get her hopes up. Being realistic about the whole thing kept her grounded, though. But weighing her résumé against the talents of Mel Cambridge between the sheets left Trina feeling a lot less marketable now.

Roscoe Hobart finally set his pen down and made a sur-

25

rendering gesture with his hands. "Let's stop all the tap dancing here and cut to the chase," he said. "There are certain things I demand from my employees and especially from my managers. First of all I want honesty at all times and loyalty to the company. If you or one of your underlings are caught stealing from this hotel, the police will be called, charges will be filed and the thief will be without a job. Period. End of discussion."

Trina told him she agreed completely with that.

He looked at her carefully for a moment. "I also won't tolerate gossip or discrimination of any kind, to include racial slurs or jokes, as well as comments about gays and lesbians or our elderly guests. This hotel wants to have full rooms. No vacancies. Who fills those rooms doesn't matter. Anyone who can pay our prices is welcome here and will be treated with respect."

Trina's ears perked up at the mention of gays and lesbians. *There's a strong possibility he has a lesbian as his assistant*, she noted as she remembered Dee Cockran's firm handshake and soft-butch hairstyle.

"Do you have any questions, Ms. LaRue?"

"A few," she said.

He set his pen down and gave her his undivided attention.

"I understand the pay would be the same for me," Trina said.

He nodded.

Trina liked that a lot. In a way it would be a raise of sorts. Her current salary would go a lot further in San Antonio than it did in Dallas.

"The job is yours if you want it, Ms. LaRue."

Their eyes met again and he seemed to be saying much more to her. *That was quick,* Trina thought. *Almost too quick. That little loyalty speech earlier was aimed directly at me. He's probably concerned that I know he cheats on his wife. His distaste for gossip was the first thing he mentioned,* she reminded herself. *He wants to make sure I don't tell anyone about Mel Cambridge!*

"Are you still interested in working for me?" he asked.

"Yes, of course."

"As I said earlier, your application stands out above the others. You have the training and the experience I'm looking for."

That made her feel better. Now it was time for her to give him the speech she always gave a future new boss. Life was too short to be in the closet at work. She would never do that again.

"There's also one more thing I'd like to get out in the open right up front, Mr. Hobart," Trina said. "I'm a lesbian," she continued, "so I hope you meant what you said about there being room for everyone here. This can be the one and only time we ever discuss it, but I want no surprises down the road. My work will speak for itself."

He seemed pleased with her honesty. Roscoe Hobart smiled for the first time since the interview began. "It already has. You'll fit right in with us. When can you start?"

Chapter Four

"So tell me what you would have done," Trina said to her Aunt Reba and Juanito as she sat down at their kitchen table. Juanito was fresh from the shower with his thick, graying hair still damp, but neatly combed. "You walk in on two people having sex in a hotel room," Trina continued, "and then the next day you discover you have a job interview with one of them. What would you have done the minute you realized who was there to interview you?"

Reba had been working in her garden and still had on her gloves and floppy hat. She began to howl with laughter as she put her hat on a hook by the kitchen door. Juanito choked and sputtered on the big drink of water he had just taken.

"Lord have mercy, girl!" Aunt Reba said. "No one gets into a mess the way you do!"

"Tell me what you would have done when you finally came face to face with him again," Trina said. She loved hearing her Aunt Reba laugh this way. The three of them were now doubled over and slapping their hands on the kitchen table.

"Maybe you should've said something like 'I didn't recognize you with your clothes on,' " Juanito suggested, which set them off in another fit of laughter. "So are you going to elaborate on this job interview?" he asked. "We're getting distracted with all this talk of walking in on those two having sex."

Trina smiled. "Nothing gets past you."

There was silence for a moment, then Reba said with exasperation, "Well? Did you apply for a job here or not? Or were they just holding the interviews here for a job at another location?"

Trina laughed. "I applied for a job here. It was an interesting interview."

Juanito started to chuckle again. "I'm sure it was! Especially after seeing him with his pants down. What did he say when he saw you?"

"Lord have mercy, that must've been embarrassing," Reba added. "Did you just catch him naked, or in the act of . . . of . . . whatever?"

"In the act of whatever," Trina said dryly. Not wanting to get into that again, she gave them a thorough description of the interview and her first impressions of a clothed Roscoe Hobart. "He was so quick to offer me the job that it made me suspicious," she admitted. "I'd caught him in a compromising position with one of the other applicants, for crissakes! It made me wonder why he would even consider hiring me."

"Maybe that's *why* he hired you," Juanito suggested. "To keep you quiet."

"Or maybe you were the most qualified person for the job," Reba said reasonably.

Trina nodded. "That's an interesting concept, but since when does one's qualifications matter once sex becomes a factor?"

"Well, did you ask him why you were selected?" Juanito queried.

"Not exactly," Trina said, "but I did ask a few staff members some questions after my interview. Then I found the desk clerk who had given me the wrong room the day before. I felt like he owed me a favor, so we had a little chat."

Trina went on to explain how after her interview she had seen Joseph in the lobby talking with one of the valet attendants. Joseph agreed to meet her at the food court at River Center Mall across the street. Once they were there, he got a table for them at a busy Starbucks where they talked for nearly an hour. Trina asked him some very pointed questions and Joseph gave her what she hoped were honest answers.

"You've never heard of the Hobarts?" Joseph asked her.

"I've heard of them," Trina said. "Roscoe is the General Manager of the Regal Palace River Walk and Nelda manages the Regal Palace River Center. They work across the street from each other and probably carpool everyday. That would be the extent of my knowledge about them, and that last part about the carpooling I made up."

Joseph smirked. "That's all you've heard? Nothing about them personally? And they don't carpool, by the way. That would be too middle class for those two."

"No, I haven't heard anything about them personally. Why? Should I have heard something?"

Joseph linked his fingers together and popped his

knuckles. "The Hobarts have an agreement between them. He likes the ladies and she likes the men. Did you meet Dee Cockran this morning?"

Trina smiled and nodded. "Yes, I did. Does she by chance play softball?"

Joseph laughed. "She's family, all right. She also mud wrestles at a club in Austin on Saturday nights, but that's a whole different subject. I'll take you there sometime if you like."

Trina imagined the look on her face was what had made him smile before he continued.

"Mr. Hobart has an agreement with his wife that he will hire as many lesbians as he can to work for him. Mrs. Hobart has an agreement with her husband that she will hire as many qualified gay men as she can find to work for her. That's how they stay out of trouble with their staff and each other. Fewer opportunities to fool around."

Trina looked at him and waited for the punch line. When Joseph didn't appear to have anything else to say, Trina muttered a simple, "You're kidding, right?"

"Serious as a heart attack." Joseph sipped his coffee and waved at a Starbucks customer standing in line to place an order. "Nelda Hobart's secretary is a flaming queen who keeps her informed about everything happening at that hotel. And I mean everything. You can't get close to her without him right there at her side. Our little Dee Cockran is the same with old Roscoe." Joseph tossed his hair away from his eyes. "I can't complain about Dee or Roscoe or really anyone else on the staff. A lot of lesbians work there. It keeps Roscoe in line and his wife out of the way. When Nelda Hobart is happy, we're all happy. When she makes his life miserable at home, he brings it to work and passes it around. It's not pleasant."

Trina was beginning to see things more clearly now, and wasn't sure how she felt about any of it.

"So tell me what you know about Mel Cambridge," Trina said. She reasoned that Roscoe Hobart wasn't entirely "in line" if he was sleeping with Mel Cambridge.

Joseph sipped more of his coffee and then ran his fingers through his hair again. It was too long, but that seemed to be the style now. Trina didn't like the way it was constantly hanging in his face, but it was better than that shiny bald look men were adopting.

"She's from Houston and thought the job was hers," he said. "Mel and Roscoe go back a ways. They've worked together before, and from what I understand, Ms. Cambridge is one of the reasons that the Hobarts have this 'gay hiring' deal going on between them now."

"Does Nelda Hobart know that Mel applied for the position here?" Trina asked.

"Don't know the answer to that. All I know is that Mel never had a chance. Roscoe wouldn't have hired her."

He slept with her, but wouldn't have hired her, *Trina* thought. "How many applicants applied for this position?" she asked.

"Just five, according to what I've heard Dee say. It became vacant quickly and there wasn't a lot of time to find a replacement. They wanted to promote from within. The other three candidates were interviewed earlier this week. Once they received your paperwork, though, it was like the search was over. I remember when Dee got your application. It was like their prayers had been answered. You were qualified and it's common knowledge that you are gay. Everyone knows everyone else's business, as you'll soon discover."

Trina wasn't too happy with that bit of news.

"Who were the other applicants?" she asked.

"The assistant F & B manager in El Paso, but he's a twerp and Roscoe doesn't like him. He's kind of cocky and wouldn't fit in well here. The assistant F & B manager from the Palace in Laredo and one from Austin. But from what I've heard, you're the most qualified and the Palace that you're coming from does very well."

Trina shrugged. Okay, *she thought.* So maybe I am the best qualified. *She had held the same position at the downtown Regal Palace Hotel in Dallas for over three years. Trina had worked her way up through the ranks in the hotel business, having previously held desk clerk and auditor positions. After honing her bartending skills in the hotel lounge on the weekends, her interests eventually turned to the food and beverage aspects of hotel management.*

Joseph set his coffee cup down on the table. "I'm not sure you believe everything I've told you so far. Are you up to another walk? I'll introduce you to FiFi."

Trina laughed. "Who is FiFi?"

"Nelda Hobart's secretary. He's great fun. You'll love him! And he'll back up everything I've told you."

Trina smiled and shook her head. "That won't be necessary, but thanks anyway."

"Well, if you get a chance, go over to River Center and check out the staff. You'll see family everywhere. I worked there for about five years. Two of my exes still work there, that's why I'm at this other hotel now. Too many cat fights, if you know what I mean."

Trina wouldn't have readily assumed that he was gay at first, but now that she had spent more time with him, there were things about him that were obvious . . . things like how he gave his head a little toss to get the hair out of his eyes and the way he held his coffee cup with a pinkie slightly extended wasn't the most masculine way to drink coffee. She did, however, like his sense of fun and his willingness to share information. Trina was looking forward to working with him.

"Are you taking the job?" *he asked.*

Trina nodded.

"Then welcome. It's an interesting place to work and most of the people like what they're doing. You'll fit in nicely."

"This FiFi person sounds interesting," Juanito said. Reba and Trina both laughed.

"I won't be working with FiFi," Trina said. "He'll be at the hotel across the street from mine."

"Then you're definitely taking the job," Juanito said.

"Yes, I'm taking the job."

Trina went back to the hotel and took a nap. She was staying in San Antonio two days to spend more time with Rosalie. Her flight back to Dallas was the next morning.

A ringing telephone woke her up at about four that afternoon. "How did your meeting go this morning?" Rosalie asked.

Trina hadn't told her the meeting had really been a job interview. "It went well," Trina said. "Better than expected, actually. How was your day?"

"Long. I spent most of it thinking about last night," Rosalie said. "You wouldn't believe the number of people who made comments about the amount of smiling I've been doing today."

After they hung up, Trina decided to take a quick shower. She would tell Rosalie about the new job and see what kind of reaction she got from the news. Trina was nervous about bringing up any of this. So far the long-distance aspect of their relationship was working nicely for them. Whenever they saw each other, it was like a mini-honeymoon. The sex was hot, and there was always something to talk about, and things to catch up on, even though they spoke at least twice a day on the phone. Maybe being physically located in different cities was what was making the relationship work so well. On another level, Trina wasn't sure she was ready for anything more than what they already had. She did have to admit she never liked seeing Rosalie leave after they'd spent time together. Trina was forever counting the days until they could be together again. None of this was ever discussed between them though, very much like the situation with Rosalie and Arty. Trina wasn't sure about how much contact Rosalie and Arty were having. Rosalie never mentioned him. The subject didn't come up between them, but the questions always seemed to be there.

She switched off the hair dryer and put on a clean, baggy T-shirt and a pair of comfortable shorts just before answering the knock on the door. Rosalie came in carrying the same small suitcase she had brought the day before.

"So I get you for another night?" Trina asked with a shy smile. Rosalie was in her arms kissing her.

"Unless I can talk you into staying longer." They continued kissing against the closed door. Trina felt weak in the knees when Rosalie slipped her hand under her T-shirt and rubbed her bare breasts. "I've thought about you all day, baby," Rosalie said. She kissed her deeply again and then whispered, "All day."

My God, Trina thought while they kissed their way to the bed. *She has me weak all over!*

Trina got in the center of the bed and moved pillows out of the way while Rosalie took off her shoes, pantyhose and light pink lacy underwear. She was wearing a brown full skirt and a white slip. Rosalie helped Trina with her T-shirt and then she straddled Trina's body. Trina looked up at her and saw the desire in Rosalie's eyes.

"Take everything off," Trina said huskily. She wanted to feel her again . . . feel her and share in the lust and adoration surrounding them. She wanted to taste her and make her quiver until Rosalie collapsed from exhaustion.

She reached up, unbuttoned Rosalie's blouse and then found the lone button fastening the skirt in the back. She slid the zipper down, and watched as Rosalie pulled the skirt over her head. The blouse joined Trina's T-shirt on the floor, and then the slip came over Rosalie's head and was tossed somewhere near the television. They both fumbled with Rosalie's bra only seconds before it too was discarded.

With Rosalie still straddling Trina's body, her knees resting on either side of her breasts, Trina felt so happy she thought she might cry. She filled her hands with Rosalie's warm, soft breasts and couldn't stop smiling.

"Come up here," Trina said. With her hands on Rosalie's hips, Trina urged her forward. "Hold onto the headboard for support." She watched as Rosalie tentatively followed instructions. Trina moved down the bed until her mouth was where she wanted it to be. She reached for a pillow and got her head propped up.

"Oh, God!" Rosalie said. She lowered herself onto Trina's mouth. "Oh, God this feels good," she said breathlessly. "Don't let me hurt you."

Rosalie leaned her body forward, allowing her knees and the headboard to support her weight as she rode Trina's tongue. Trina kept one arm around Rosalie's hips, still urging her forward, pulling her closer so Rosalie could grind herself into Trina's face where eager lips and a probing tongue were waiting for the chance to please her. Trina moved her other hand around the front of Rosalie's body and squeezed her nipples. Rosalie began to move faster then, up and down against Trina's tongue. A deep, guttural sound rumbled in Rosalie's throat seconds before she began to wildly thrash and bounce her way toward an orgasm. It seemed to last an amazingly long time as she gripped the headboard and shivered at the pleasure racing through her body. Rosalie let her knees hold her up while Trina continued to slowly lick and suck her there. Trina could feel Rosalie quivering with new, tiny orgasms as she explored her this way. Finally, Rosalie raised up on her knees and pulled herself away from Trina's glistening face. Rosalie lay down beside her and put her head on Trina's chest. Trina reached for the sheet and dried her mouth and chin.

"That was out of this world," Rosalie whispered in a trembling voice.

Trina kissed the top of her head. "You liked it?"

"Oh, my God," Rosalie said as she hugged her tightly. "Oh, my God," she whispered.

Chapter Five

Trina woke up hungry at about seven-thirty that evening. Rosalie's arm was around her where they had ended up falling asleep spooning. Trina turned over and kissed her awake.

"I'm hungry," Trina said. "For food this time."

Rosalie smiled and stretched sleepily. "This time?" The sheet slowly slid down her body and uncovered her breasts. Trina couldn't stop herself from kissing them.

"So what sounds good for dinner?" Rosalie asked. She held Trina's head in her hands and guided her lower so that she could take more of her breast into her mouth. "Room service again? Getting dressed and going out? Burgers? Ordering a pizza?"

Trina was now fully involved in Rosalie's body once more. She wasn't quite as hungry for food as she had thought.

"I can't seem to get enough of you," Rosalie said as she pulled Trina on top of her. They shared a deep, passionate kiss and then Rosalie wrapped her legs around her. As the kiss became more intense, they slowly moved against each other until a nice, steady rocking motion began. Trina raised herself up with her arms and arched into her, increasing their connection. Rosalie put her hands on Trina's back and added her own deliberate grinding movements. It wasn't long before Rosalie came and squeezed her legs even tighter around Trina's lower body to make the most out of what was happening. Her desperation to prolong the feeling and the intensity made everything perfect for Trina. She responded to Rosalie's soft "ohhs" and the hot, bold way she rubbed against her, demanding attention. Had Rosalie not been so determined to get all she could at that moment, Trina wouldn't have been able to come again. Rosalie's momentum and desire seemed to carry Trina over the edge.

Trina finally stopped moving, and just rested on top of her for a moment. She could still feel herself throbbing and didn't want to do anything to make it stop. Her brow was damp. She liked the way Rosalie pushed hair away from her forehead to kiss her there.

"Is it usually like this between women when they make love?" Rosalie whispered.

Trina lay beside her and took Rosalie into her arms. Rosalie nuzzled her neck. "You mean hot and sweaty?" Trina teased her.

"No," Rosalie said and gave her a playful swat. "I mean is it always this good?"

Trina shrugged. "I've never had bad sex with a woman, if that's what you're asking."

"Oh." Rosalie moved her hand so that she could touch Trina's breasts. "No, that's not what I was asking, but now that you've brought it up, how many women have you been with?"

Trina chuckled and suddenly felt embarrassed. "A few."

"How many is a few, in your opinion?"

"Why would you want to know?"

Rosalie moved her hand under Trina's breasts and then slowly brought it up to touch her chin with her index finger. "I just do."

Trina opened her mouth and took Rosalie's finger gently between her teeth. Trina's stomach made a loud grumbling noise that caused them both to laugh.

"Let's go eat," Rosalie said. "We can finish this conversation over dinner."

Trina suggested they eat downstairs at the hotel restaurant. She wanted to check out the menu and the employees there. As the new Food and Beverage Manager, the hotel lounge, restaurant and room service would be her responsibility.

"What's good here? Do you know?" Rosalie asked as she studied the menu.

"Right now it all looks good," Trina said. Her stomach growled again to emphasize her point. The selections were typical hotel restaurant cuisine with a nice mixture of "south of the border" to give it local flavor. Trina steered away from that for now and decided to sample a steak instead. She wanted to see how good the meat supplier was.

They placed their orders. Trina was amused to see that their waiter was not only friendly, but gay. She glanced around to take in more of the ambiance of the dining room.

"Hello?" Trina heard someone say. She blinked and then noticed Rosalie waving a hand in front of her face.

"Where are you?" Rosalie asked.

"I'm sorry," Trina said sheepishly. "Did you say something?"

"We were going to continue our earlier discussion. The conversation where you tell me about all your old girlfriends."

Trina glanced at her watch. "Do we have that much time?"

"Oh, that doesn't sound good!" Rosalie said with a laugh.

Trina smiled, but suddenly felt a little nervous. To do this correctly, they would both have to exchange ex-lover stories. Trina wasn't ready to hear anything about Arty yet. The other men in Rosalie's life before Arty were less intimidating to her, but still she worried. Trina had been involved with several straight women, and learned early to stay emotionally unattached. At first, Trina had been confused and off balance a lot of the time, and tended to forget that for most of them, affairs with women helped spice up their marriages or fulfill some fantasy they had harbored their entire lives. Trina had been able to separate the love versus sex factor when dealing with them, but when Rosalie came into her life, insisting she was now a lesbian, Trina had not accepted that information easily. She was still making the effort to disassociate herself from Rosalie's past. For Trina, her acceptance of Rosalie as a lesbian was still a work in progress.

"Well?" Rosalie said.

The waiter returned with their decaf coffees. Trina took a sip and knew immediately what one of her first changes would be. *The removal of caffeine shouldn't make coffee taste weak,* she reminded herself. A lesson on how to properly make coffee would be at the top of her list.

"*Well?*" Rosalie said again, dragging the word out a bit longer than was necessary.

"If we get into the ex-lover discussion, it'll take away from the news I have," Trina said.

"What news might that be?"

Trina set her cup down. "I have a new job and it begins in two weeks. I'll be relocating to another city."

Rosalie's face paled almost immediately. She sat back in her chair, and looked at Trina, then down at her coffee cup.

"Wow," she said quietly. "This is kind of sudden."

Trina shrugged. "The job came open quickly and I applied for it."

"Two weeks," Rosalie said with a sigh. She folded up the napkin that had been in her lap and set it between her silverware and coffee cup. "Where is this job? Are you staying in Texas or at least a bordering state? Louisiana? Oklahoma? Does Arkansas even have a Regal Palace Hotel anywhere?"

"I'll be staying in Texas," Trina said as she noticed the tears welling up in Rosalie's eyes. Trina felt even more nervous now. This was such a huge step for her . . . for both of them. She would be returning to San Antonio with the possibility of being constantly reminded of her parents and the humiliation they had made her go through. There would also be more opportunities to see the rest of her family, as well as old family friends who had sided with her parents' decision to disown her. Word about Trina's sexual orientation had spread quickly after she had been forced to leave home. Even though years of therapy supposedly had prepared her to deal with things like her family's rejection, it wasn't that simple. Trina had worked through all of her fears of rejection, and overcome the self-esteem issues that had nearly crippled her emotionally. She had felt mentally strong and healthy for a long time now, but the thought of returning home and possibly having to deal with these issues again was weighing heavily on her mind.

"What did I order?" Rosalie asked. "I'm not very hungry any more."

"Pasta with shrimp," Trina said.

"That's right." Rosalie sighed again. "You didn't answer my question. Where are you moving to? Houston, El Paso, Laredo? Corpus has fewer flights and is about a two hour drive. Dallas wasn't as —"

"I've been offered a job here in San Antonio," Trina said.

"At this hotel. It's the same job I have now in Dallas. This one came open and I interviewed for it this morning."

Rosalie's eyes were suddenly huge. She opened her lovely mouth to say something, but no words came out. Trina was relieved to see her smiling again even though Rosalie was blinking back tears. Trina took a deep breath, telling herself everything would be fine. Her parents and her brother would continue to be jackasses and never accept her for who she really was, but she had other people in her life who would make up for that.

"You see that man over there by the fountain?" Trina said. "The man in the blue suit?"

Rosalie looked where Trina had indicated and then nodded.

Trina took a sip of weak coffee and said, "I saw him naked yesterday."

Rosalie unconsciously ran her fingers through Trina's hair as she held her. They had just finished making love again and were winding down for the night. Trina felt relaxed and safe, and liked the way Rosalie kept touching her as they got comfortable in bed.

"I've never *ever* seen my boss naked," Rosalie said after a moment.

"I wish I could say the same."

Through dinner they had talked about Roscoe Hobart and his wife. Eventually, they got back to the subject of Trina's moving back to San Antonio. Trina managed to postpone that discussion a while longer, but apparently Rosalie wasn't about to let her get away with that for long.

"Why didn't you tell me the reason you were in town?" Rosalie's voice was soft and sleepy.

"I wasn't sure I'd get the job," Trina said. "There didn't seem to be any point at the time."

"But just the fact you would consider moving here," Rosalie said. "Doesn't that mean something significant? Or am I the only one seeing it that way?"

"It could be significant," Trina agreed. She closed her eyes, listening to Rosalie's heartbeat. Rosalie had the nicest chest and shoulders that Trina had ever rested on.

"*Could* be significant?" Rosalie repeated. "What does that mean?"

"My Aunt Reba is getting older," Trina said. "I haven't spent enough time with her these last few years."

"So you're moving back to be closer to your Aunt Reba." It wasn't a question.

"Well, it's not the only reason."

Rosalie brought her hand over and slowly, gently began touching Trina's breast. The caress was a light fluttering at the nipple and made Trina want to burrow deeper into the softness of Rosalie's body. Occasionally Rosalie would take the nipple between her thumb and index finger, then go back to the light butterfly caresses. It didn't take long for Trina to begin to squirm and press against her. She was tingling all over and absolutely loved this kind of attention.

"What other reasons could there be?" Rosalie whispered.

Trina kissed Rosalie's shoulder and upper chest. "I see two very nice reasons right here."

"Oh, really?" Rosalie asked. She filled her hand with Trina's breast and then returned to lightly teasing the nipple again.

Trina smiled and hugged her. "Juanito also misses me, you know," she said quietly.

"I see. Juanito, Aunt Reba and my breasts. Nothing else?" Rosalie moved her hand up and touched Trina's hair again.

Just being with you is the best reason of all, Trina thought as they both drifted to sleep. *The best reason of all . . .*

ROSALIE

Chapter Six

At first Rosalie was curious about the way Trina never wanted to talk about anything personal, but after the incident with the job interview and Trina's struggle to share such an important decision with her, Rosalie began to see things differently. She started having doubts about Trina's ability to make any kind of commitment, no matter how small it was. She also noticed how often Trina would change the subject when Rosalie tried to get any type of answer from her about how she felt about their relationship.

For Rosalie, the turning point in her life had been the moment she realized she didn't love Arty and wanted his sister instead. She became a changed woman, expecting to be taken seriously as a lesbian, and eventually, as a lover. Rosalie now considered herself to be a lesbian. She wasn't sure what all it entailed, but she was in love with another woman. It never occurred to Rosalie that Trina would have so many concerns about being with someone who hadn't been out very long. Trina's behavior, however, made it difficult for Rosalie to see this any way other than something negative. Trina obviously wasn't in love with her, but Rosalie felt certain that Trina did have strong feelings for her. Even though she hadn't admitted it yet.

That was the other thing that had caught Rosalie's attention — how Trina seemed to be able to turn off her feelings so quickly. At no time since their first kiss three months earlier had Rosalie gotten the impression that Trina wanted or needed to be with someone. Rosalie always initiated the sexual part of their relationship and most of their communications. From what Rosalie could see, Trina's attitude about the whole thing was rather ho-hum until they actually got into it. Rosalie saw Trina as a controlled, quiet person who carefully kept her emotions in check. Even after three months, Rosalie didn't feel she knew Trina any better now than she did the day they met.

Rosalie also decided it would serve no purpose to dwell on Trina's need for so much privacy. Taking it personally would do no good. Rosalie wasn't the clinging, possessive type, but an occasional hint that she was desired when they were someplace other than bed was something everyone needed at times. Trina was an attentive lover, and Rosalie felt as though their time together had been good for both of them. Rosalie hoped with enough love and patience, they could work through whatever issues Trina had as far as intimacy was concerned. In the meantime, Rosalie herself had a few problems of her own to deal with that seemed to be taking up a lot of her extra energy.

Her efforts in keeping the lines of communication open with her parents, after having canceled her wedding to Arty LaRue, were still an on-going affair. Coming out to them, and giving a reasonable excuse for breaking off the engagement, were two of the hardest things Rosalie had ever had to do. She and her parents were making progress in coming to terms with all of the changes. A firm believer in positive reinforcement, Rosalie had dinner with her parents at least once a week, but spoke to each of them on a daily basis. She made it a point to bring up Trina's name often, and keep them posted on whatever lesbian or gay activities Rosalie herself was interested in. Rosalie was adamant about bringing this part of her life to the forefront where her family was concerned. She refused to let them hide from the fact their daughter was now a lesbian.

Rosalie had embraced her new lifestyle with unabashed enthusiasm. After having done research on the local gay and lesbian organizations, she was surprised to discover how conservative the gay community was. Being curious about this new part of her life wasn't getting her very far, but she remained realistic enough to know she would now be spending her time in the closet if she wanted to keep her job and many of her current friends. Rosalie's parents, however, were a different matter. She would continue to have their love, but she also wanted their support in the lifestyle she had chosen. They were slowly coming around, but it was taking a bit more work than she had first thought it would.

Rosalie's mother called her earlier to invite her to have dinner with them at the Outback Steak House. Tonight seemed to be as good a time as any to tell them about Trina moving to San Antonio. The fact she knew nothing about Trina's plans was still somewhat unsettling for her. Rosalie was reluctant to suggest she and Trina move in together. In addition, she didn't feel comfortable asking her questions about the arrangements Trina was making for when she finally did arrive in town. Trina's unwillingness to share things with her was something else Rosalie wanted them to work on.

Over dinner Rosalie and her parents kept the conversation

safely generic. Everything was going well until Rosalie mentioned possibly teaching summer school in order to pay back the money her parents had spent on the wedding that had never taken place. Rosalie felt bad about having ruined everyone's plans and she wanted to get it off her conscience, but her father still wasn't cooperating.

"We don't want your money," Peter Cofax said. "Take the summer off and relax. Enjoy yourself. That's why we all became teachers, remember?"

"I'm doing it anyway," Rosalie said. "I want a clean slate. I still feel awful about all of this."

Alicia Cofax closed her menu. "We're just glad you came to terms with things before you got married. The LaRues don't seem to be a very forgiving family. There's no telling what kind of life you would have had if you'd gone through with the wedding."

"I'm dating their daughter," Rosalie reminded her. "I'm not out of the woods yet, I'm sure." That seemed to quiet them down a little. "In fact, Trina is moving here to San Antonio. She's transferring to one of the Regal Palace Hotels downtown."

"Oh, really?" Mr. Cofax said. "Will we finally get to meet her?"

Rosalie smiled. He was trying so hard.

"Yes, you will. Soon, I hope."

"How long has it been since you've seen Arty?" her mother asked.

Rosalie hoped her parents weren't secretly thinking that she would come to her senses and get married. Occasionally she caught them exchanging a look that seemed to be saying, "Let's give this some time. She'll be her old self again in no time."

"He hasn't shown up at my apartment in almost three weeks," Rosalie said, "and since I've changed my telephone number, he doesn't call me anymore."

"Are you sure he's not following you?" her father asked.

Rosalie was careful whenever she was out alone, no matter what time of day or night it was. Being aware of her surroundings was second nature to her since her older brother had become a police officer. He had preached so often about safety for women Rosalie felt she would know if Arty, or anyone else, had been following her.

"I'm sure he has a new girlfriend," she said. "There's no reason for him to follow me."

"You practically left him at the alter, dear," her mother reminded her. "Arty never struck me as the kind of young man to give up so easily."

Arty hadn't taken the news of the broken engagement well, and had hounded her for weeks. She had been honest with him up to a point, stating she no longer loved him, but hadn't bothered to tell him she was in love with his sister instead. After having fallen in love with Trina, Rosalie had come to realize this was actually the first time she had ever really been in love before. She had cared deeply for Arty when they had decided to get married, but knew now she had never been in love with him.

"Hopefully he's found someone who can give him what he wants," Rosalie said. The guilt about having hurt him still gave her a few sleepless nights.

"I was looking forward to having a plumber in the family," Peter Cofax said with a teasing smile. "Arty never got around to fixing that leaky faucet in the guest bathroom."

Rosalie smiled, wondering how much of her father's profession Trina had absorbed as a child. "Maybe the plumber's daughter can fix it for you," Rosalie said. She was relieved when both of her parents laughed.

Checking the directions she had scribbled on the back of an envelope, Rosalie turned the radio off when she finally found the street she was looking for. It was a nice neighbor-

hood, with "Good Neighbor Watch" signs on a few street cor-
ners. She found the address Naomi Shapiro had given her on
the phone several days ago. There were three cars in front of
the house. Rosalie pulled into the driveway and parked behind
a Toyota pickup.

"You must be Rosalie," the dark-headed woman said. She
held the door open for her. "Come in. I'm Naomi Shapiro. We
spoke on the phone."

Rosalie followed her down a hallway into a huge living
room where an older man her father's age and another
woman who was Rosalie's age were sitting on opposite ends
of the sofa.

"Did you have any trouble finding the place?" Naomi
asked.

"Not really," Rosalie said. "You gave me great directions."

"Make a name tag. We have them over there on the table."

Rosalie had found the Lesbian and Gay Teacher's Support
Group listed at the Community Center. She called to get information and spent nearly thirty minutes talking to Naomi
about the group.

"What is it you teach?" the other woman asked. According
to the label stuck to her blouse, her name was Cricket and
she taught eighth-grade history.

"Second grade," Rosalie said.

"Oh, isn't that a fun bunch?" Cricket said. "You get them
before they think they know everything."

The man came over and introduced himself as Ron. His
name tag identified him as a geometry teacher. "I'm the token
male for the group." He poured himself another glass of Coke.

"I had this huge crush on my second grade teacher,"
Cricket said. "We used to have to lay down and take a nap for
about twenty minutes every day. I remember one day we were
on our pallets and the teacher walked by and began tiptoeing
between us to get something from the back of the room."

Cricket covered her mouth to suppress a giggle. "She had a dress on and I saw her underwear."

Everyone laughed and Rosalie finally began to relax. She helped herself to the selection of appetizers and poured a soft drink from one of the opened bottles on the table where the name tags were.

"After that," Cricket said, "I never took another nap at nap time. I was on the lookout for the teacher's underwear."

"Even then you liked older women, eh?" Naomi said.

Cricket giggled again. "I think you're right!"

Naomi went on to explain to Rosalie that Cricket's lover just happened to be her best friend's mother.

"And she's a hottie," Cricket said.

The doorbell rang, and three other women arrived. They were all regular members of the group and knew each other, but made name tags and each introduced herself to Rosalie. It was the first time Rosalie had ever been around so many gay people at one time. She felt empowered and less lonely. Rosalie imagined such an organization would help teach her how to handle a career in a homophobic atmosphere. She wasn't sure what else a support group could offer her. She wanted to prepare herself for any unpleasantness waiting for her down the road. In this respect, Rosalie became a student again and listened to everything these people had to say.

Naomi started the discussion off by stating how much easier it was when there was more than one gay teacher in a school.

"It just makes for a nicer working environment," Naomi said. "Cricket and I teach at the same school. We're pretty sure the Phys Ed teacher is a lesbian, but she's married."

Light laughter made its way around the room.

Cricket snorted. "Naomi and I spend most of our free time trying to catch her doing something dykey, but she's gone to a lot of trouble to avoid us this year."

"It's not like we're following her around or anything," Naomi explained, giving Cricket a mock-stern look.

"But we do things like check and see if she's scheduled personal days off during the Dinah Shore Golf Tournament or women's week at Ptown," Cricket said.

To be polite, Rosalie laughed along with everyone else, but had no idea what was so funny. To her relief, Ron asked the questions that Rosalie had been too embarrassed to ask.

"Dinah Shore Tennis Tournament?" Ron said. "Ptown? I need to recruit more guys for this group. I can't break the code alone."

All the women except Rosalie burst out laughing.

"It's the Dinah Shore *Golf* Tournament," Cricket said. "Not tennis. And Ptown is actually Provincetown, Massachusetts, the lesbian capital of the world."

"Well, excuse me," Ron said with a laugh.

Rosalie was soaking up all this information and filing it away for later. So far she hadn't been able to break the code either, but with the help of her computer she would definitely be doing some research on the LPGA Tournament schedule and Provincetown, Massachusetts!

Chapter Seven

Rosalie hoped she didn't seem too eager when Naomi asked her to stay a while longer after the meeting was over. Cricket stayed as well, and the three of them cleaned up from the meeting while they talked.

"We think it's important to get feedback from new people who attend these things," Cricket said. "It's a big step for most people to try something new and we want to make sure you come back."

"Frankly, this has been an eye-opening experience for me," Rosalie admitted. "In more ways than one. I'm dealing with two entirely new issues here so it's been interesting."

Naomi consolidated all the remaining appetizers onto one

plate and then filled up three new plastic cups with ice and Caffeine-free Diet Coke.

"Sit down and let's talk about these issues," Naomi suggested.

"That's what we're here for," Cricket said. "We call this a support group for a reason. I also think it's important to the group that someone representing elementary education is involved with it. You bring a different perspective to the meetings. Some of the kids you teach will eventually realize they are gay. This is a very important time in their lives so in a way the risks for you can be greater if it's discovered that you're a lesbian."

"My parents are both teachers," Rosalie said. "That was one of their main concerns when I came out to them recently. What if my boss were to find out or some of the parents? These are all new concerns for me." She was embarrassed to admit she had only known she was a lesbian for three months. Even though Trina hadn't been any help at making her feel all right about it, Rosalie was pleased to see that Naomi and Cricket were delighted she was trying to learn everything she could.

"We all had to start somewhere," Naomi said. "You'll learn what to say, and what not to say, when you're talking to co-workers."

Cricket even told her how lucky she was to have discovered it so early in her life. "Some women never figure it out."

Rosalie sighed. "So I'm here for many reasons," she explained. "I know nothing about being a gay teacher and even less about being gay. The terminology and the inside lesbian jokes . . . like the LPGA and something as simple as the lesbian capital of the world," she said. "I want to know everything. I want to break the code!"

All three had a chuckle over that. When Rosalie left two hours later, she had successfully completed a course in Lesbian 101. Naomi loaned her a copy of *The Lesbian*

Almanac, two lesbian romance novels and a copy of *The Well of Loneliness.*

"These are classics," Naomi had told her. "You'll be an official lesbian if you read them."

Cricket gave Rosalie a pat on the back as they walked out to their cars. "I bet you didn't think you'd leave this meeting with homework!"

Rosalie read *The Price of Salt* and *Curious Wine* in three days, in addition to working and spending time with her parents. She had trouble putting the books down, excited to find such literature existed. *The Well of Loneliness,* however, was another matter. It was depressing, so she took breaks with it and spent more time reading *The Lesbian Almanac* instead. Determined to break "the code", Rosalie soaked up as much as she could.

"Did you know that gays and lesbians have their own flag?" Rosalie asked Trina on the phone one evening. Trina was still in Dallas, but would be moving very soon.

"Yes, I knew that," Trina said.

"Do you know what each color on the flag stands for?"

"Why would I need to know that?" Trina asked with a chuckle.

"A good lesbian would know."

Trina's laughter was low and husky. "Then I guess I'm a bad lesbian. The red stripe goes on top. That's all I need to know."

Rosalie could hear the amusement in Trina's voice as she continued.

"How much do you know about flag etiquette in general?" Trina asked. "I'm a firm believer that when we have a gay flag that's flying upside down, we have a homosexual somewhere in distress. Isn't that the gay rule?"

After being subjected to Trina's teasing, Rosalie decided to stop sharing her gay/lesbian knowledge with anyone. She would just continue to pay close attention when she was at a support group meeting and become a good lesbian on her own. She also ordered her own personal copy of *The Lesbian Almanac* and returned Naomi's books to her at the next meeting.

Trina arrived the day before her furniture. Rosalie was confused about why Trina insisted on staying with her Aunt Reba instead of at Rosalie's apartment. It was a Friday afternoon when her cell phone rang while she was stuck in traffic on the way home. Trina invited her over for dinner at Reba and Juanito's house.

"When did you get in?" Rosalie asked. When they had talked the night before, Trina hadn't mentioned she would be in San Antonio the next day.

"A few hours ago."

Rosalie waited several seconds for more guidance on how the evening was expected to go — would she be spending the night there at Reba's with Trina? Would the two of them go back to Rosalie's apartment? Was this just an invitation to dinner and nothing more? Rosalie's frustration was snowballing, but she didn't know what to do about it. As intimate as she and Trina had been over the last three months, Rosalie felt she knew nothing about this woman other than she was in love with her. Rosalie wanted more than amazing sex. She needed to know that she meant something to her . . . that she was at the least worthy of knowing what Trina's living arrangements were going to be!

"So that's where you'll be staying tonight?" Rosalie finally asked.

"I still have a bedroom here," Trina said. "Aunt Reba has kept it looking the same all these years."

Rosalie's disappointment and anger were escalating. She wanted to see her so badly, but didn't think Trina felt the same way. The car behind her honked. She looked up to see the light was green.

"What time should I be there?"

"Dinner will probably be ready around six," Trina said, "but you can come over any time."

Remembering again that they had talked last night on the phone and Trina hadn't mentioned that she would be in San Antonio today, Rosalie began to feel like an afterthought . . . nothing more than an acquaintance or a friend. Rosalie didn't know what to say or how to even broach the subject of how this was affecting her. They never talked about things like that or made any plans for the future. Rosalie was beginning to wonder what role she was supposed to be playing in all of this. *Will things ever get better*, she wondered. *Is this what all lesbian relationships are like?*

"When can you be here?" Trina asked softly.

Finally, the traffic was beginning to move. Once again Rosalie was confused, and then to hear her say something like, "When can you be here?" in that low seductive tone . . . Rosalie was beyond confused. She was hurt and disappointed.

"Are you okay?" Trina asked.

"I'm fine," Rosalie said, fully aware that she didn't sound fine at all. "I need to go home and change clothes," she said. "What can I bring?"

"Just you."

"My mother raised me better than that. I'll pick up dessert and can probably be there in an hour." Rosalie made a decision right then. She wouldn't stay the night with Trina this time. They had to talk soon. There would have to be some changes. If this relationship was nothing more than sex for Trina, then Rosalie had to decide what to do about it. She felt tears on the way, and told Trina she would see her shortly.

* * * * *

Rosalie gave Juanito the box with the chocolate cream pie inside. He and Aunt Reba were ready with warm hugs for her. Juanito looked the same with his thick, neatly combed gray hair, chinos and a brown T-shirt. Reba wore her fine gray hair up in a French braid and had on blue slacks and a flowery print short-sleeved blouse. Rosalie had only met Reba and Juanito one other time, when she and Trina had gone out to dinner with them for Juanito's sixtieth birthday. Rosalie had liked them both right away and enjoyed their humor. Reba and Juanito were retired teachers, so there had been an instant rapport between them. Juanito had taught high school Spanish for thirty years; Reba had taught Chemistry at the same school. All three shared many of the same interests. Rosalie loved thinking about retiring some day, and hoped she would be as prepared for it as these two seemed to be.

Trina came out of the kitchen and kissed Rosalie on the cheek. "Can I get you something to drink?"

Just seeing her made Rosalie's heart skip a beat. Hearing Trina's low, husky voice in her ear sent tiny chills racing down her arms.

Aunt Reba volunteered to get their drinks and named off what they had available. "You two have a seat. I'll be right back."

Trina took Rosalie by the hand and led her to the sofa in the living room. In her tan shorts, slim brown belt, sandals and a denim short-sleeved blouse neatly tucked in, Trina looked both relaxed and elegant. Rosalie was still upset.

"How was your day?" Trina asked. They were sitting next to each other and Trina rested her arm on the back of the sofa, touching Rosalie's hair as she spoke.

"My day was fine," Rosalie said. She couldn't bring herself to ask about Trina's day. She didn't even want to know. Everything was becoming more clear to her now. If Trina didn't see her as important enough to share information with, then Rosalie didn't like what this meant. She stood up and straightened her skirt. "I need to go see if they want any help in the kitchen."

"Things are fine in the kitchen," Rosalie heard Trina say behind her.

At the kitchen door she took the glass that Reba handed to her. "What are we having?" Rosalie asked Juanito.

He lifted a lid from a steaming pot and announced, "Chicken with rice. My specialty."

"It smells delicious!" Rosalie said. "Anything I can help you with?"

"Everything's almost ready."

Rosalie asked Reba about her garden, and Reba eagerly led the way out the back door to give her a tour. The more Reba talked, the more calm Rosalie began to feel. She looked up and saw Trina standing at the back door watching them. Rosalie's stomach did a little flip the moment their eyes met, but she also felt a slow uneasiness. She still had no idea what Trina was thinking. It was as though she didn't exist for this woman outside of the bedroom.

"You're supposed to plant squash on little hills and corn in a circle," Reba said, "but I prefer everything in a row. It's easier to keep the weeds out that way."

The back yard was big and shady, with a swing under an oak tree and a grape arbor on the other side of the garden. Juanito and Trina came outside together, laughing. The ice in their glasses clinked as they made their way down the back porch steps.

"Are we ready to eat?" Reba called.

"You can help me set the table after I take a look at my watermelon plants and my sunflowers," Juanito said. "Trina thinks gardening is a big waste of time," he said to Rosalie. "She says it's cheaper to just go to a store and buy everything."

"We don't garden to save money," Aunt Reba said. "We like fresh vegetables. And it keeps me active. How much

61

exercise do you think retired people would get if they didn't have yards and gardens to piddle in?"

Once Juanito was satisfied the snails hadn't gotten to his crop yet, he motioned for Reba to follow him back into the house. "Help me set the table," he said. "Dinner's almost ready."

Rosalie was about to offer to help them when Trina asked if she would join her on the swing.

"Please sit with me for a minute," Trina said.

They slowly walked toward the swing. Rosalie sat down next to her and was surprised when Trina reached for her hand.

"You're upset about something," Trina said. "Tell me what it is."

"We'll talk about it later. After dinner."

"Is it bad? Does this have anything to do with Arty?"

Rosalie looked at her. "Arty? Why would you think this concerned Arty?"

Trina let go of her hand. "It feels like everything has to do with Arty."

They both looked up when Reba called to them from the back door. They went into the house in silence, but Rosalie was even more confused than she had been earlier.

Chapter Eight

Dinner was more entertaining than Rosalie initially thought it would be. The food was excellent and the conversation centered around Aunt Reba and Juanito's various teaching experiences. When Rosalie told them about the Gay and Lesbian Teacher's Support Group, they were as excited as Rosalie had been. She answered as many of their questions as she could, and when Aunt Reba inquired about whether or not retired teachers were welcome at the meetings, Rosalie promised to find out.

"I've learned a lot and it's been great fun," Rosalie said. "They not only care about being there for each other, but they share ways to help gay students when it's possible. Sometimes a kind word at the right time can change a child's life. In the upper grades, many gay students are out at school."

"It's not easy growing up gay," Trina said.

Rosalie glanced over at her. On impulse, she reached for Trina's hand and gave it a reassuring squeeze.

"I had a little boy in my class last year who liked to draw pictures of men and boys wearing lacy aprons," Rosalie said. "I never thought too much about it until I started attending these meetings."

"I had one of those aprons on just before you got here," Juanito admitted with a grin.

Everyone laughed.

"You watch that little guy," Juanito said to Rosalie. "His best friends are probably girls, and before you know it he'll be wanting to do their hair."

After dinner, the four of them went to the living room for coffee and dessert. They continued talking until Reba and Juanito got sleepy.

"We'll leave you two young things alone now," Reba said. "Make yourselves at home. We're getting up early and hitting some garage sales in the morning."

Juanito yawned and stretched. "Like we don't have enough crap of our own already."

"One man's crap is another man's treasure," Reba said on her way down the hall to her bedroom.

Rosalie could hear them fine-tuning their plans for the next day before they said goodnight to each other. Their bedrooms were across the hall from each other. Once she and Trina were alone, Rosalie took that as her cue to leave as well. She picked up her purse and pulled out her keys. "Thanks for inviting me to dinner," she said. "It was nice seeing everyone again."

"Where are you going?" Trina asked.

They looked at each other for a long moment. Rosalie could see the surprise in Trina's eyes.

"I'm going home," Rosalie said as she straightened her skirt.

"Why are you leaving?" Trina asked. She also stood up. "You're angry. I think you even arrived here angry. Talk to me, Rosalie. Please don't do this. Tell me what's happened."

"It's what hasn't happened that's the issue, Trina. I don't want to do this now. We'll talk about it another time."

"I want to talk about it now," Trina said.

"You don't always get what you want." Rosalie opened the front door and hurried down the sidewalk to her car. As she got in, Rosalie could see Trina standing on the porch with the door open behind her. *You'll be able to handle this better tomorrow*, Rosalie reminded herself. *You're way too emotional right now.*

All the way home Rosalie kept going over everything that had happened during the last three months. Trina's ability to shut her out of even the smallest events surrounding her life was suddenly overwhelming for her. *It's not even like she's saving these things to surprise me*, Rosalie thought as she cried. *She's keeping absolutely everything from me. And for what? Is it a power trip? A way of reminding me that I'm not important enough to share things with?*

Rosalie parked her car in front of her apartment. When she went inside, she heard her telephone ringing. It stopped as soon as her answering machine kicked in. About twenty seconds later, the phone rang again. Rosalie answered it without even checking the Caller ID.

"Hello?" Rosalie said.

"I can't believe you just left that way," Trina said.

"I'm sorry, but I thought it was best."

"You were supposed to stay over here tonight."

"When were those plans made?"

There was silence for a moment. "I assumed you would stay here tonight," Trina said.

"Did you? Well, we've both been assuming a lot of things lately."

"Have we? What kinds of assumptions have you been making?"

Rosalie was tired and her emotions were raw. "I assumed I would know when you would be officially moving," she said. She took off her shoes and got comfortable on her sofa. "I assumed I would know if you were to ever take a job in San Antonio. I assumed I would know if you cared about me anywhere other than in bed and I assumed I would know if I meant anything to you. So we both have been assuming too much."

There was more silence on the phone before Trina finally said, "Wow. Where did all of that come from?"

"Silly assumptions," Rosalie whispered. That was all it took for her to begin crying again. There was no way to disguise what was happening; the tears were evident in her voice. Finally, she said, "I can't talk about this now."

"Rosalie —"

"Please, Trina."

"You're crying," Trina whispered. "My god, Rosalie. We need to talk about this."

"I know," Rosalie said with a sniff, "but not now. Maybe tomorrow."

More silence, then Trina said, "If that's what you want."

"I'm tired and I'm going to bed. Maybe I'll feel better

tomorrow." Rosalie hung up the phone and checked her messages. There were seven blinking lights, all hang-ups.

All from Trina trying to reach her earlier.

Rosalie woke up to her doorbell ringing. She squinted at the clock and saw it was nine-thirty already. She never slept that late on the weekend. Her internal clock almost always had her awake at six and up and around by seven.

As someone continued to ring the doorbell, Rosalie found her robe and struggled into it while shuffling to the door. Looking through the peephole, she could see a delivery man with a long narrow box. She asked who it was and he told her he was from Flowers To Go. Rosalie opened the door and took the box he handed to her.

"Thank you," she said with a yawn. She signed where he pointed and then closed the door. Now fully awake, Rosalie slipped the small card from under the bow and read, *Let's talk today. Call me.* It was signed by Trina and had a phone number written under the signature. Rosalie brought the box of flowers up to her nose and inhaled the sweet scent of roses. She put them in a vase and called the number on the card. Trina answered the phone immediately.

"You sent me flowers," Rosalie said. On the other end of the line she could hear Trina's deep sigh.

"I was afraid you wouldn't call."

"Why would you think that?" Rosalie asked.

"You were so different last night. I've never seen you that way before."

"I've been letting things go lately in hopes they would get better," Rosalie said. "They haven't. The roses are beautiful, by the way. Thank you."

"Can you come over? Or can I take you to breakfast? What time is it anyway?"

"It'll be closer to lunch by the time I get ready," Rosalie said. "Are you free for lunch?"

"Am I free? Of course, I'm free. Can you come over here?" Trina asked. "Or I guess I could meet you somewhere."

Rosalie named a restaurant. She didn't want to get distracted by being alone with Trina before they had a chance to talk. She knew they would end up in bed and not get anything resolved.

"The flowers really are beautiful," Rosalie said again as she leaned closer to the vase and buried her nose in them again. "Roses are my favorite."

"I remembered you telling me that once," Trina said quietly.

Rosalie smiled. "You're such a romantic, Trina LaRue. I'll see you in a little while."

Rosalie arrived at the restaurant and saw Trina sitting in her car, waiting. She was beautiful and had a young, sporty look about her. Dressed in light green shorts and a yellow shirt, Trina carried herself with confidence.

They met on the sidewalk where Rosalie gave her a hug. Once she got closer Rosalie could see how tired Trina looked, but even so, Trina was still a strikingly beautiful woman.

"How are you?" Rosalie asked.

"I'm glad to see you." Trina opened the door for them. "I didn't sleep well last night."

They were shown to a table right away and given menus.

"Was I the reason you didn't sleep well?" Rosalie asked.

Trina lowered her menu just enough so Rosalie could see her eyes. "Yes," she said simply. "Would you have called me had I not sent you the flowers?"

"I would have been in touch eventually," Rosalie said. "I didn't have Reba's telephone number, but I would have tried your cell phone."

The waiter came and took their orders. When he left, Rosalie noticed that Trina wasn't looking at her and was slowly drumming the fingers of her left hand on the table.

"What are you thinking?" Rosalie asked.

Trina took a deep breath. "I'm trying to figure out what happened last night. Then I keep asking myself if I really want to know." She looked up and Rosalie saw the confusion in her expression. "How are things right now?" Trina asked. "With us, I mean."

"If you're thinking the flowers did the trick and I'm going to forget the other things I've mentioned, then you need to think again. That isn't going to happen."

"Then I'm not sure this is a good idea," Trina said.

Rosalie felt a sinking sensation in the pit of her stomach. "What isn't a good idea?"

"Us meeting this way."

"You have something else in mind?" Rosalie asked. "A better idea? Another place where we can talk?"

Trina didn't say anything. Rosalie decided that she wouldn't do this alone. If Trina wanted to continue seeing her, then she would also have to get involved with the things that were less pleasant than making love. Communication was vital to any relationship, and Rosalie refused to be without it now.

"This isn't getting us anywhere, you know," Rosalie said. "I've told you about my concerns and all you chose to do is try and fix it with flowers."

"What is it that you want from me, Rosalie?"

"I told you that last night. I want to know about things that affect both of us. The job, the move, when you'll be in town, where you're going to stay while you're here. I think I made that pretty clear last night. You don't tell me anything, Trina. Anything."

The silence was back and continued until their food arrived. It remained with them through most of their meal until Rosalie finally spoke up again. "So you have nothing to say?"

"You're making absolutely no sense to me," Trina said evenly. "I thought you would like spending time with me, then you throw a little fit last night and drive off into the night without giving me a reason."

Even though her voice had been low and calm, Rosalie could see Trina's hand trembling as she held her fork.

"If this has anything to do with Arty, I need to know now," Trina said. Her voice trailed off toward the end of the sentence. Rosalie watched her as she picked up her water glass and took a slow drink. Trina's hands were still shaking.

"Does it?" Trina asked.

"Why would you think any of this had anything to do with Arty?" Rosalie asked.

Trina shook her head and went back to finishing her lunch. She didn't say another word even though Rosalie attempted to ask more questions. After another long, awkward silence, Rosalie finally told her she couldn't stand this any longer.

"You can't stand what?" Trina asked.

"Call me when you're ready to talk, Trina."

"I was ready to talk last night."

Rosalie collected her purse and put some bills on the table.

"Don't you dare walk out on me again," Trina said.

"I meant what I said, Trina. I can't do this anymore. When you're ready to listen to me and hear what I have to say, we can talk. I mean really talk. That's the only thing that will fix this. Not flowers and not dinner with your family nor lunch on a Saturday afternoon. You know where to find me." Rosalie had to leave the restaurant before she started to cry again. Once she was in her car and pulling out of the parking lot she felt more sad than angry.

Chapter Nine

Rosalie was disappointed but not really surprised when she didn't hear from Trina later Saturday afternoon or even Saturday night, but when Sunday afternoon came around and she still hadn't heard from her, Rosalie had another good cry. Needing to get out of her apartment, Rosalie arranged to have dinner with her parents. Before seeing them, however, she decided to find someone to talk to about the situation with Trina. She called Naomi Shapiro and asked her if she had some time to talk.

"It's personal," Rosalie told her on the phone. "It has nothing to do with the support group. I understand if you're busy or have plans already, but I really need some advice."

"Sure," Naomi said. "Can you come over now?"

It was such a relief to have something to do. The waiting had taken its toll on her. Rosalie was beginning to think maybe she was making a mistake wanting Trina to take some responsibility for their relationship. *But if you give in now,* she thought, *it'll always be this way between us and this is totally unacceptable.*

Just driving across town made Rosalie feel better. It had been a long day, and she wasn't exactly sure what she should do next. Rosalie had felt so alone. She hated that she had been waiting for Trina to get in touch with her. She also wasn't happy about having to call a mere acquaintance for advice when she had so many other friends, but Rosalie hadn't told anyone besides her family yet that she was a lesbian. That made it more difficult to judge who her real friends actually were anymore. She felt isolated, and hadn't expected that. Trina had warned her against coming out to any of her co-workers; Rosalie's parents had practically told her the same thing. That whole situation made her almost as depressed as this new crinkle in her relationship with Trina.

When she arrived at Naomi's house, two other vehicles were parked out front. Sensing this wasn't a good time after all, she was slow to get out of her car. *Maybe this is a bad idea,* she thought suddenly. *Here I am parading my personal life around in front of a virtual stranger.* However, she rang the doorbell. She needed some guidance. Once she made the decision to call Naomi, a rush to get some insight became her main priority. Rosalie still wasn't clear on how lesbian couples did certain things, and she considered Naomi a voice of reason, as well as someone experienced. Naomi had mentioned once that she and her lover had been together nearly two years already. *Just a few questions*, Rosalie thought. *I'll just ask a few questions.*

Naomi answered the door with a smile and a warm welcome. "Come in. Cricket and a friend are here to measure my bedroom for some new furniture I'm buying."

"If this is a bad time —"

"No, not at all," Naomi said. "Come in. Can I get you something to drink?"

Rosalie greeted Cricket, and was introduced to another woman. Her name was Carmen Morales. She appeared to be in her mid-fifties. She held an impressive-looking measuring tape as big as her hand and had a pencil stuck behind her left ear. She wore blue jeans with creases down the front and a blue denim shirt with the sleeves rolled up. Carmen waved absentmindedly in Rosalie's direction and then handed Cricket the pencil, motioning for her to follow her into another room.

"We can talk in here," Naomi said as they went into the kitchen and climbed on stools at the breakfast bar. "What's up?"

Rosalie put her head in her hands and felt at a total loss for words. "I don't even know where to start."

"It sounds like girlfriend trouble," Naomi said quietly. She handed Rosalie a glass of ice and a Caffeine-free Diet Coke.

Rosalie popped the top on the can, filled her glass and nodded. "It's just that I'm so new at this. I don't know if I'm expecting too much from her or if I'm just in love with a woman who is destined to make me crazy."

Naomi's chuckle made Rosalie relax a little. It felt good to be doing something constructive. If this visit could help clear up anything for her, Rosalie vowed to do whatever she could to help the support group.

"Start at the beginning," Naomi said. "How did you meet her?"

Cricket and Carmen came into the kitchen chattering. Carmen announced that the new furniture would fit fine and asked when Naomi wanted it delivered.

"Oh," Cricket said. "Are we interrupting something?"

Rosalie sighed. "Girlfriend trouble. I'm wandering around in unfamiliar territory here and need some advice."

Getting two more sodas out of the refrigerator and passing them around, Naomi said, "All of us can probably relate to that. Do you mind if they stay for this?"

"I can't vouch for how helpful my advice would be," Carmen said, "but I can surely offer you an opinion."

"My track record hasn't been that great with women until recently," Cricket admitted. "No guarantees here either. Can we stay anyway? I just *love* dyke drama."

"I'll take all the help I can get," Rosalie said. "I've already thrown my pride out the window and there's a chance you can help me make some sense out of what's happening in my life."

"So tell us where you met her," Naomi said, "and tell us her name."

The three other women perched themselves on stools and gathered around the breakfast nook in the kitchen. They sipped their drinks and listened as Rosalie told them how she and Trina had met.

"It was Christmas Day actually," Rosalie said. "Just four months ago. At the time I happened to be engaged to her brother."

Cricket let out a hoot. "Ohmigod! Really?"

Rosalie laughed. The other three laughed with her.

"Way to go!" Cricket said. "Merry Christmas to Rosalie!"

"Well, tell us what happened," Naomi said.

"So, four months ago you weren't a lesbian?" Carmen interjected.

Rosalie shook her head. "This woman swept me off my feet and wasn't even trying."

"Damn!" Cricket muttered under her breath.

"So you met on Christmas Day. Then what happened?" Naomi asked again.

Now that Rosalie had their attention, she felt embarrassed.

"I thought I loved him," Rosalie continued, "and I felt it was time to get married. Arty and I had been dating for over a year and we were spending Christmas with his parents."

She went on to explain how Trina's arrival at the house that day had been a complete surprise to her. "I had no idea that Arty had any siblings. He'd never mentioned anything about having a younger sister."

"Was it love at first sight?" Cricket asked quickly. "Did she make you want to hang around under the mistletoe when she was in the room?"

"No, not at first," Rosalie said to an escalation of laughter.

"When did that part happen?" Cricket asked. "Okay, okay," she said when Naomi and Carmen both gave her similar *please be quiet* looks. "I'll shut up. Continue."

Rosalie went on to tell them how Trina had arrived that day with a bag full of presents while she was wearing a T-shirt that said: Nobody Knows I'm a Lesbian.

"I learned later that she only wears that shirt on Christmas Day, and only when she's visiting her parents," Rosalie explained.

More laughter filled the kitchen. "I like this woman already," Naomi said. "So you two hit it off right away?"

"Not really," Rosalie said. "I didn't get to see much of her that day. She only stayed about five minutes. Just long enough to drop the presents off and get her parents all riled up. Then she left."

"What did she say to get them upset?" Carmen asked.

"Nothing really," Rosalie said. "Just the fact that she was there at all seemed to do it. She's not welcome in their house, but they always seem to let her in on Christmas. They strongly disapprove of her lifestyle. Get this," Rosalie said. "She comes in and greets everyone and she even knows all about me, which was a complete surprise. In the meantime, I'm standing there wondering who she is. Her parents are mad and Arty is pacing. I'd never seen him so agitated before. Trina comes in and kneels down beside the Christmas tree. She then takes four beautifully wrapped gifts out of the bag she has with her. She gets up and moves back out of the way and stands there with her arms folded across her chest. She's standing there watching as her father yanks up his present and goes to the front door, opens it up and tosses his gift out on the lawn."

"He *what*?" Cricket said with an incredulous cackle.

"Oh, it gets better," Rosalie said.

"Her father actually threw his present out the door?" Cricket asked.

Rosalie nodded. "I'm standing there wide-eyed and a little frightened. I wasn't sure what to expect next. Then I watch as her mother snatches up her present and does the exact same thing. I stood there stunned as Arty picked up his gift, followed his mother to the front door, and he pitched his present out on the lawn."

After a moment of shocked silence, Naomi asked, "What did Trina do?"

Rosalie took a sip of her drink and then shook her head again. "She just stood there watching them with me. It finally occurred to me that all four of them were waiting for me to do something. Trina had brought a present for me as well and each and every one of them were staring at me now. It was awful."

Carmen chuckled and also shook her head. "What happened next?" she asked.

Rosalie smiled at the memory. "Trina leaned over and said, 'Need help with that? Want me to throw it out for you?' "

More howling laughter filled the kitchen.

"Is this for real?" Cricket asked. "Did this really happen?"

"Could anyone make something like this up?" Carmen wondered aloud.

"I say run, Rosalie," Naomi informed her. "These people are weird as hell."

"That's crossed my mind more than once," Rosalie admitted. "Anyway, that was Christmas Day. After Trina left, I got the deep dark family secret out of Arty. It seems Trina came out to her parents when she was in high school and they kicked her out of the house. She went to live with her aunt on the other side of town. She lived there until she graduated from college. She only sees her parents and her brother for a few minutes every year on Christmas Day. I felt awful for her and I was embarrassed that I hadn't known what had been going on within the family. I was about to marry into all of this. That day I saw a new side to Arty." Rosalie was quiet for a moment before saying, "I took it upon myself to ask Trina to be in the wedding."

Naomi smiled. "That was a nice thing to do."

Rosalie shook her head again. "I thought so, too. I think I'm a fixer by nature. I just wanted everyone to get along. But when the LaRue's found out about it they swore they wouldn't attend the wedding if Trina was in it. They felt so strongly about things, her father said he wouldn't go even if Trina *attended* the wedding, much less became a member of the wedding party." Rosalie shrugged. "I took that as a challenge and set out to help patch things up between them."

"So you didn't change your mind about her being in the wedding?" Cricket asked.

"No."

Cricket giggled. "Then fast forward to the good part where the lesbian bridesmaid kisses you for the first time."

More hoots of laughter filled the kitchen. "Quite the opposite happened," Rosalie said. "I found myself calling her several times a day to talk. She lived in Dallas then, by the way, and we began corresponding by email and talking on the phone all night long. Trina came down from Dallas several times to help me take care of some wedding details like dress fittings and shopping for various things for the reception." Rosalie stopped for a moment, then smiled again. Her voice became much softer when she continued. "I couldn't stop thinking about her. She was so much fun to be with and we could talk about anything. I'd call her the moment I woke up in the morning and it was her voice I wanted to hear before I fell asleep every night. I couldn't wait to check my email as soon as I got home from work everyday to see if she had written to me and I would get so excited when I knew she would be in town for something." Rosalie looked up at the three women sitting across from her. "I didn't feel any of that with Arty. I began having trouble talking to him and relating to him. I was a confused mess. But the entire time this was going on in my head and my heart, I kept up with the wedding plans! The wedding was my link to Trina. That was my excuse to keep calling and flirting and . . . and everything. I continued to order flowers and arrange for the caterer and I booked the band and sent out invitations until it finally hit me that I was not in love with Arty. There was no way I could marry him. I was in love with his sister."

There was another long silence before Cricket said, "Awww." She reached over and gave Rosalie's hand a squeeze and then asked, "Who kissed who first?"

"I kissed her first," Rosalie said.

"Way to go, Rosalie!" Cricket high-fived each of them.

"But not before giving Arty his ring back, canceling the wedding and telling my parents that I was a lesbian."

"Wow," Carmen said. "Did you stretch all of that out over a day or two? Or do it all at once?"

"All in the same day," Rosalie said, feeling somewhat depressed as the memory returned to her. The look on Arty's face when she gave him back his ring was still fresh in her mind. He had done nothing to deserve being hurt that way. "It was awful," she said and took another deep breath. "But I had to do it. I couldn't approach Trina with any of this until I had settled things with Arty and gotten out of the wedding."

"What did you do after that?" Naomi asked.

Rosalie was more relaxed now that the most embarrassing part of the story was behind her. "It was a Friday night and already getting late. I drove to Dallas and spent four hours practicing what I was going to say to her."

"Well, was she happy?" Cricket asked. "Was she proud of you for standing up to Arty and your parents? None of that could have been easy. What did she say when she saw you?"

"I called her when I got into town because I had no idea where she lived. She found me, and I followed her home. When I finally got around to telling her what I had done and why I was there, she didn't believe me."

Naomi was the only one who laughed this time. "Hey, just think about it. I wouldn't have believed you either."

Rosalie nodded. "I know. We ended up having words and she made me angry so I tried to leave her apartment. She kept taunting me and telling me to go back to Arty. That it probably wasn't too late to patch things up with him." Rosalie felt numb at the memory of that night and how Trina had showed her no mercy. "The way it started out was not pretty," she admitted.

"How did it end up?" Cricket asked quietly.

Rosalie was able to smile then. "I was hopelessly in love by the time morning came around."

Chapter Ten

Rosalie was amused at Cricket's attempt to get more details out of her in reference to her first night alone with Trina. The questions were helping her deal with some of the anxiety she was feeling. After each question that Cricket posed, all four women would burst out in hearty laughter. A red-faced Rosalie finally admitted that the sex had been incredible and she had never once regretted her decision not to marry Arty.

"I came to terms with my sexuality almost overnight."

"That's amazing," Carmen said.

"So where do things stand with you and Trina now?" Naomi asked.

Rosalie went on to explain about Trina interviewing for a job in San Antonio and how secretive she had been about it.

"Nothing," Rosalie said. "She told me nothing about it until after she got the job."

"I might have done the same thing," Carmen said reasonably. "Why get your hopes up about something that might not happen?"

"If I thought that were the case," Rosalie said, "I would agree with you, but I'm sensing something else from her. Anyway, that was two weeks ago. In the meantime I've been waiting on word about when she would be moving here. Then Friday afternoon she called me to say that she was here and then she invited me over to her aunt's house for dinner."

"How did that go?" Cricket asked.

"The dinner went fine," Rosalie said in frustration, "but that was hardly the point!"

"Then what is the point?" Naomi asked.

"Are you upset because she's not telling you things like the job interview or when she'll be in town next?" Carmen asked. "Or is it something else?"

"I hate not knowing what's going on with her and with us! Am I being unreasonable about that? Why do I have to be the last to know about something that affects my life, too? That's the basis for our recent argument, but are we arguing if I'm the only one talking about it?"

"I hate it when people won't argue when I'm ready," Cricket said. "That pisses me off even that much more."

"Do you two argue a lot?" Naomi asked.

"Not at all. This is the first one we've had. It's occurred to me," Rosalie said glumly, "that mostly we just have sex. We don't talk about things. I ask questions and she ignores them and never answers me."

"Well, that's not good," Cricket noted. "Sounds kind of like a guy."

"You said you needed some advice," Carmen said. She ran her fingers through her thick, salt and pepper hair. "What is it you think you need help with in particular?"

Rosalie shrugged. "I keep trying to compare this with

what I know about men. Everything else about my relationship with Trina has been wonderful. The sex, the intimacy, the way we can share things and have the same interests. We've read the same books. We like the same old movies. We listen to the same kind of music. All of that has been such a nice change from what I was used to with the men I've dated over the years."

Naomi nodded. "But you have questions about what? How it should be in a lesbian relationship?"

Rosalie nodded. "Are the dynamics the same? I expect to feel closer to her than I did to Arty, but in many ways I don't. It's like she won't let me get close at all, at least not in a way other than the physical. She doesn't tell me things that I think I have a right to know. She doesn't share her feelings, even though I've asked her to over and over again."

"She doesn't tell you things like what?" Cricket asked.

"Things like where she's going to live when she moves to San Antonio. Things like where she'll be staying while she's getting settled! It makes me furious when I think about her staying with her aunt instead of me. It was never an option for her. I had no say-so in that decision. No input into any of it."

"Did you ask her to stay with you?" Carmen wondered.

Rosalie stopped to think for a moment. "Well, no." When the other three laughed Rosalie added, "But she never told me when she would be here. She moved without letting me know! I didn't really feel comfortable bringing it up before then."

"Did you two argue over this?" Cricket asked. "Have you told her how you feel? What you want?"

Rosalie covered her face with her hands again. She was getting a headache. She got two Tylenol out of her purse and took them.

"Friday night at dinner over at her aunt's house I was upset that she had moved already and hadn't told me,"

Rosalie said. She went on to explain that they had talked the night before, and Trina hadn't mentioned anything about moving the next day.

Cricket shrugged. "Okay, that's a little weird."

Rosalie continued. "Trina invited me over for dinner Friday after work. Imagine my surprise at having her in town without some sort of advanced announcement! I just felt so left out of everything," she said with a sigh. "I wasn't sure why she wanted me there. I was almost certain she expected me to spend the night with her at her aunt's house, but it wasn't made clear. I made up my mind before I went over that I wouldn't be staying, though. Trina didn't like that at all and we ended up having words before I left."

"So did you ask her why she's being so secretive about all of this?" Naomi asked. "Maybe she has good reasons or a valid explanation."

"Has the 'C' word been used yet?" Carmen asked.

"The 'C' word?" Rosalie looked at Naomi. "More of the mysterious lesbian code?"

"Commitment," Carmen explained over light laughter. "Have you two discussed that? Or are you just dating?"

"I'm in love," Rosalie said flatly. "I'm in this for the long haul."

"How does Trina feel about that?" Cricket asked. "How long of a haul is she in it for?"

"She's changed jobs and moved here," Naomi pointed out. "That's a good sign."

"I can't get her to talk about it," Rosalie said. "Friday night when I left it wasn't under the best of circumstances. I told her how disappointed I was at being the last to know everything. She wanted me to stay with her that night and I wouldn't."

"Does she understand how you feel?" Carmen asked.

"I don't think so," Rosalie admitted. "Even though I've

explained all this to her several times now. Yesterday morning she sent me a dozen long-stemmed roses. We met for lunch and ended up not speaking afterward."

"The roses were a nice touch," Cricket said. "I have to admit she sounds kind of controlling. What degree on the butch scale is she?"

"Butch scale?" Rosalie asked. She again gave Cricket and Naomi her *is this another part of the lesbian code you're going to make me break on my own* look.

"You know," Cricket said. "Is she a soft butch, hard butch, foo-foo butch . . ." She then made a motion with both of her hands as if presenting Carmen to an audience of thousands. "Or a *butch* butch?"

Naomi, Cricket and Carmen laughed out loud. Rosalie looked at all three of them as if waiting for the rest of the joke.

"What the hell is a foo-foo butch anyway?" Carmen asked Cricket.

"You know," Cricket said. "Has her nails done but wears a tool belt. Or even better . . . she wears a pink tool belt."

"Sorry," Rosalie said. "You've lost me again."

Carmen shook her head. "It's okay. She lost me, too."

"Let's get back to Rosalie's problem here," Naomi said. "Where are things with you and Trina now?"

"I left her at the restaurant on Saturday afternoon when she refused to talk to me about any of this. I've been waiting for her to call me since then, but I've heard nothing."

"Uh oh," Carmen said. "Did you two break up?"

Rosalie looked at her with a puzzled expression. "No. Of course not."

"Are you sure?"

"Wouldn't I know if we had?"

Carmen shrugged. "I don't know. Would you? Looks like you didn't know anything about the new job or the move."

"In my mind we haven't broken up," Rosalie said. "We're just having a misunderstanding."

"What about in her mind?" Carmen asked. "To me it sounds like you've broken up."

Cricket tossed a thumb in Carmen's direction. "That's the way a butch would see it."

Carmen ignored her. "She sent flowers and that didn't work. There are questions you want answers to and she's not talking. Cricket's right. That's controlling behavior. If you wait around for her to call you, it might not ever happen. Trina might see it as she's already made the first move once. She sent you flowers. That was an apology for whatever it was you think she did."

"I've told her what she did," Rosalie said. "And it's more about what she *didn't* do than what she did do. She never talks about anything. I don't want that. Am I asking for too much?"

"That depends," Naomi said. "Some people can't open up. She might've been this way all her life."

Cricket agreed with that. "I guess I'm still confused about what you expect from her and how we can help you."

Sounding defeated and weary, Rosalie said, "Just having someone to talk to is helping. I don't have any gay friends. I don't feel quite so alone even though it's like I'm rowing up stream and getting nowhere." She folded her hands on the breakfast bar in front of her. "So what should I do next?" Rosalie asked. "I can't have her thinking that we've broken up, so it sounds like I need to go see her. Do I insist that she talk to me about these things that are upsetting me? Or do I try and forget about them and just get over it?"

"I think —"

"Oh!" Rosalie said. "I just remembered something else that struck we weird yesterday at lunch with her. She asked me if this had anything to do with Arty. That sort of came out of the blue."

"Ahh," Naomi said. "What's your relationship with Arty now?"

"He was harassing me for a while. I had to change my

phone number, but it's been about three weeks since I've heard from him."

"She might be jealous of Arty," Carmen said. "After all, you almost married him. I would assume that you and Arty slept together."

Rosalie's face turned a bright shade of red.

"That's a very safe assumption, Sherlock," Cricket stage-whispered in Carmen's direction. "They were getting married."

"She's jealous of Arty," Carmen said simply. "Jealousy can make us do a lot of things that we would never do under regular circumstances."

"I'm in love with her," Rosalie said. "I was finished with Arty before anything happened between me and Trina."

"Have you told her that you're in love with her?" Naomi asked.

Rosalie stopped to think for a moment before saying in a near whisper, "Things are just so good between us when me make love. I know how she feels just by the way she touches me. I guess I've assumed that she would know the same thing about me and how I feel toward her."

"Then here's my suggestion," Cricket said. "It's all kind of simple. You need to go see her right now and tell her how you feel. That's the first thing you have to do. Then see what happens from there."

"Would that be a problem?" Naomi asked her.

Rosalie shook her head, feeling uneasy about the possibility of already having experienced a breakup. That had never occurred to her before Carmen mentioned it. What if Trina was out with someone else right now? What if she had old girlfriends in San Antonio that were available? Rosalie felt a sense of urgency about wanting to get in her car and drive over to Reba's house and get this whole thing straightened out as quickly as possible.

"The other thing is," Carmen said, "you can't be worrying about if you're doing the right 'lesbian thing' or not. There's

86

no right or wrong way to do something in situations like this. Each relationship is different. Some lovers live together and some don't. Some lovers pile all their money in one checking account and some don't. It all depends on the couple and the people involved. You two have to do what's right for you."

"Marcel and I have our own homes," Naomi said, "but we're together almost every night at either her place or mine when she's in town."

"That's why she needs new bedroom furniture," Cricket said, nodding toward Naomi. "They've worn out the other set already."

"You liar!" Naomi said with a laugh.

"I really appreciate this," Rosalie said as she got off the stool. "You've all been very helpful."

"You can count on us any time," Cricket said. "Bad advice is always free with me."

"We want to know what happens!" Carmen said. "I'll be thinking about this for days now."

"I'll keep in touch," Rosalie promised.

Once she was in her car she called her mother and explained that she couldn't meet them for dinner after all. She made a date for later in the week and drove over to Reba's house.

TRINA

Chapter Eleven

It was eight o'clock by the time the pizzas arrived. Trina paid the delivery man and gave him a generous tip. It was tradition for them to always order more pizza than they could eat at one time. Trina and Aunt Reba liked cold, leftover pizza for breakfast the next day. Juanito preferred popping his in the microwave. One pizza would more or less be gone in a matter of minutes, while the other had a life expectancy of around noon the next day.

"This is delicious," Aunt Reba said as she stretched mozzarella cheese about ten inches from the bite she had taken. "What is it about pizza that makes it just as good hot as it is cold?"

"Do you believe an old chemistry teacher is asking us that question?" Juanito said to Trina.

"Old? Did he just call me old?"

Ignoring her, Juanito went on to explain his thoughts about cold pizza. "Grease is what's holding it all together when you eat it the next day. It's like a whole different type of food when you've got cold, solid grease involved. Just think of it as nature's culinary glue."

Trina smiled. "I could have done without that cold-grease-serving-as-culinary-glue visual."

"Are you ready to begin the new job tomorrow?" Juanito asked.

"Sure," Trina said, starting in on the crunchy part of the crust. "There might be some type of orientation I have to go through, but basically I'll be in the same job, only in a different location. Learning my way around the hotel itself will probably take up most of the day."

"You've never had a problem making friends," Reba said. "I expect you'll do fine."

"Not to mention the fact there should be gay people everywhere, from what you told us about the staff," Juanito said.

Trina noticed the two of them exchanging a familiar look. Juanito got up from the kitchen table and poured himself more grape Kool-Aid. He refilled their glasses, and got himself another slice of pizza from the box before sitting back down.

"You two have something to say?" Trina asked.

"Us?" Reba said innocently. After a moment all three of them laughed.

"I can see that you're both itching to ask me something."

"We're just curious," Juanito said. "That's all. You know. The usual."

"Curious about what?"

Reba took over then. "Curious about why you were gone only a short period of time yesterday and why you were here all day today."

"Why would you be curious about any of that?" Trina

asked, teasing them. They were two of the nosiest people she had ever known. It was just one of many things that made them so much fun. "Am I cramping your style already?"

"We're retired," Juanito reminded her dryly. "We have no style."

With a shrug, Trina said, "Rosalie and I aren't seeing each other any more." She could feel all the positive energy leaking out of the room.

"I'm very sorry to hear that, dear," Reba said quietly. "I liked her. She was good for you."

Trina forced herself to take another bite of the crust. "What makes you say that?"

"The way you were when she was around," Reba said. "There were times when you would let your guard down and it was easy to see how happy she made you."

"Well, I'm not what she wants," Trina said. She took another bite of pizza and chewed stoically as she settled back into her pensive mood.

"She told you that?" Juanito asked.

"Not in so many words, but then she didn't have to."

The doorbell rang and Juanito went to answer it.

"Sometimes things have a way of working themselves out," Reba said as she reached for another slice. "Don't be so quick to give up on something you want."

"It's pretty amazing how fast things can fall apart," Trina said. She didn't want to think about this any more. She had to work on putting it all behind her and moving on. This was the way relationships had always gone for her — spurts of happiness and then nothing.

"Look who's here," Juanito announced. He came back to the kitchen with a huge grin and with Rosalie following behind him. "She didn't believe me when I told her we had enough pizza to go around."

"Pull up a chair, Rosalie!" Aunt Reba said delightedly. She opened the pizza box sitting in the center of the table and revealed three large slices there, and pointed to the other pizza cooling on the counter behind them. "Get her a plate, Juanito. We're drinking sugar free Kool-Aid, but we have some adult beverages too if you'd prefer that. What would you like? Trina can get it for you."

Trina couldn't take her eyes off Rosalie, and in return Rosalie's incredible blue eyes were fixed on Trina.

"I'll have what everyone else is having," Rosalie said.

Juanito set a plate and a glass of grape Kool-Aid down in front of her.

"I was supposed to have dinner with my parents this evening," Rosalie said as she nibbled at the pizza slice she had selected.

"Well, it's very good to see you again," Aunt Reba said. "No one here felt like cooking tonight."

Trina was so unnerved at seeing Rosalie there she couldn't eat anything else. After lunch on Saturday, Trina had finally reached a point where she could function without getting too upset. She didn't want to get any of this uncertainty stirred up again when she needed a quiet, peaceful evening before starting her new job the next day.

"The nine o'clock news is coming on soon," Aunt Reba said. "I think I'll go check it out."

"Me, too," Juanito added. They both picked up their empty plates and set them in the sink. "Last one out has to put the pizza away," he reminded Trina with a wink.

Seconds later Trina and Rosalie were alone in the kitchen. Trina was no longer hungry, still somewhat in shock.

"They can sure disappear fast," Rosalie said.

"They've had a lot of practice over the years."

Rosalie gave her a weak smile. "From all those high school and college girlfriends of yours?"

"College mostly," Trina said. "This is where we all used to hang out." She opened the pizza box on the table. "Have some more. There's plenty."

"I'm not very hungry."

Trina closed it again and put both pizza boxes in the refrigerator. "I'm surprised to see you," Trina said.

"Really? I thought you would have called me by now."

A huge weight had tumbled from Trina's shoulders. *Maybe there's still room for hope here,* she thought.

"I have a few things to say to you, Trina. Is there some place where we can talk?"

Trina went to peek out the kitchen door and saw Reba and Juanito watching TV in the living room in their recliners. There was a good chance they were dozing already.

"We can talk in here, or out on the back porch," she said. "Whichever you prefer."

Rosalie indicated the back porch. Trina left the kitchen light on so it would filter out onto the porch and in the back yard.

"Are you excited about your new job?" Rosalie asked once they got settled on the back steps.

Trina could feel the warmth of Rosalie's soft skin as their arms touched. There was an occasional light breeze that gave Trina a gentle reminder of the perfume Rosalie was wearing. She remembered how wonderful it was to be able to nuzzle her neck and hair.

"The first few days on a new job are usually the worst," Trina said. "By this time next week I'll have a better handle on things." She put her arms around her legs and then rested her chin on her knees. "What's on your mind? You were very unhappy with me yesterday at lunch."

"You noticed?"

Trina chuckled. "I noticed."

"The first thing I want to say is that arguing with you is extremely frustrating."

Trina nodded. "I've been told that before."

"Does all of that come naturally?" Rosalie asked. "Or is it something you're doing on purpose just to annoy me?"

"I don't do well with confrontations. At least not when it

has to do with personal matters." Trina lowered her voice. "In a work environment, I can be direct and a real pain in the ass when I need to be."

"Trust me," Rosalie said. "That pain in the ass thing carries over into your personal life as well."

"Okay, so I'm no fun to argue with," Trina said with a smile. "What else did you want to say?"

"I have a question to ask you," Rosalie said. "I need for you to tell me what you meant when you asked if any of this had to do with Arty."

Trina could feel her entire body get tense just from hearing her brother's name.

"I need to know what your thoughts are."

"I'm not sure I want to talk about Arty," Trina admitted.

In a calm voice, Rosalie said, "Then let me tell you something that I don't want either. I don't want there to be things between us that we can't talk about."

Once again Trina felt a tiny thrill tap dance through her heart. No one had ever said anything like that to her before.

"Now tell me what you meant yesterday when you asked me if any of this had to do with Arty."

Trina took a deep breath and said, "I know you've been in contact with him since the engagement was called off. That's been on my mind a lot. I expect you to go back to him. Maybe not today and maybe not tomorrow, but some day you will." This was the way she felt. Whenever Rosalie was away from her, Trina allowed herself to forget how they were together and focused on how she imagined Rosalie had been with Arty instead.

"You have got to be kidding me," Rosalie said. The words were spoken with a tinge of anger and surprise.

"I shouldn't have told you."

"That's what you really think?"

Trina could hear the emotion in Rosalie's voice already and she wished she had kept her thoughts to herself. *That always seems to work best*, Trina thought, as she realized, too late, these circumstances were no different than any of the others she had struggled through with an endless string of women. All different players — all the same results.

"Thoughts of you and Arty are not something I purposely set out to dwell on," Trina said in her own defense.

They sat there on the top step in the dim glow of the kitchen light. Trina was eventually lulled into a safe, easy sense of warmth and familiarity. She could hear the bugs chirping in the yard and the sound of a neighbor's stereo playing music from a Rhythm and Blues radio station. Then she heard Rosalie sniff beside her and it brought the pain back to the surface. Trina was reminded again why the truth had to be kept private and protected. It wasn't worth this and she could see now, after less than four days here in this town, it had been a mistake to move back to San Antonio.

Finally, Rosalie cleared her throat and tried to say something, but her voice wasn't there. She leaned back, propping herself up with her arms as she looked up into the dark city sky.

"Then tell me what I have to do to convince you," Rosalie said.

"Convince me of what?"

Rosalie cleared her throat again and the next time she spoke her voice sounded more normal. "How can I convince you that you're the only person I want to be with?"

Trina felt a lump forming in her throat and a swooshing sensation in the pit of her stomach that caught her by surprise. "I wish I knew the answer to that."

"I think you already do know the answer," Rosalie whispered. "I think you're using Arty as an excuse to keep some distance from me." She sat up straight and wrapped her arms around her legs again. "Arty has been in touch with me. I've never contacted him. He was calling me for a while there. That's why I had my number changed."

"I know," Trina said. "Aunt Reba told me."

"How could she know?"

"Family spies," Trina said. "No one's safe from LaRue gossip."

"Could the family gossip also confirm that I have no interest in Arty?"

Trina's weary smile was safe in the dark. "Yes, that's also been confirmed. When you told me you changed your number, Aunt Reba let me know what she heard the next day. Aunt Missy reported that Arty's old girlfriend still wasn't interested in him."

More silence followed before Rosalie finally said, "How could you ever think —"

When her voice failed her again, she stopped and started over, only louder this time. "How could you ever think that I would want to be with someone else? Especially a man and in particular Arty?"

Trina still didn't want to have this discussion. She closed her eyes, leaned back to clear her head and focused on the sounds in the back yard.

A few minutes later she heard Rosalie say, "Take your time. I'm not leaving until you answer me."

That statement gave Trina a new reason to panic. "I really don't want to talk about this."

"The bottom line, Trina, is that this isn't just about you now and it's not about me either. This is about us. So I need to have you tell me, in your own words, why you think I would ever consider being with Arty again."

Even though Rosalie was crying, her voice was strong and steady.

"I'm not some fickle teenager who doesn't know what she's doing or what she wants," Rosalie added.

"I can't help the way I feel," Trina said.

"Then *tell* me how you feel. I need to know."

Feeling trapped and frustrated now, Trina said, "Did you ever wonder why I always wanted you to visit me in Dallas instead of me flying here to be with you? Did you ever wonder why I never stayed very long when I had to be in San Antonio for those wedding details?"

"I thought you had to work," Rosalie said. "My schedule is so predictable. Yours isn't."

"My turn to ask you a question," Trina said. "When you and Arty were dating, where did you spend most of your time alone with him?"

Again the silence seemed to hang in the air between them. Trina continued.

"Arty lives at home with my parents. That leaves your place as the love den." To drive her point further home, Trina added, "I've never been to your apartment and I have no desire to go there. You can think whatever you want about me. All I know is that Arty is everywhere. He's in our lives and he's looking over my shoulder each time I touch you. The amazing thing about all of this is that when I'm with you, I'm able to forget about most of that. You make me feel loved and happy. I'm not used to having that with a lover. But as good as things seem to be with us during those times, I never hang on to the good feelings for very long."

When Rosalie reached slowly for her hand, Trina felt a tear roll down her cheek. Rosalie laced their fingers together and kissed each one separately.

"You're a real mess, you know that?" Rosalie said. "I have an idea how we can clear a lot of this up for you and for all of us. But first I need to tell you the one thing I came here to say. I'm in love with you, Trina LaRue. I want to be with you and I want to share my life with you. That's where I'm coming from. Those are the things that are the most important to me. So now you need to figure out what you want and then you need to share those thoughts with me. I have to know."

Trina's eyes clouded over with tears. She couldn't speak. She put her arm around Rosalie and pulled her close. Kissing the top of Rosalie's blond head, they stayed that way for a long time. Trina's heart finally stopped pounding. She knew somehow everything would be all right with them again. Then right there in the soft light from the kitchen, Trina could feel the magic begin when Rosalie raised her head and found Trina's lips with her own. The connection was electric and subtle.

Trina knew in her heart that Rosalie wasn't the only one in love.

Chapter Twelve

Trina felt lightheaded from the butterflies in her stomach as she and Rosalie continued to kiss on the back steps of her Aunt Reba's house. There was no way Trina could pretend she wasn't totally in love with this woman. What troubled Trina the most about this was the feeling that when good things happened to her, there were usually bad things on the way to screw it all up. Trina was afraid to give in to it . . . afraid to leave herself open to the possibilities Rosalie had so easily hinted at. Trina saw herself as a coward when it came to love or giving or even something as simple as honesty in a relationship. But Trina had been brutally honest earlier in the evening, and Rosalie was still there. Rosalie was with her, kissing her and touching her. Trina was helpless to do anything about it, and when she stopped fighting those feelings of eventual doom, she finally let herself be swept away with emotion. The knowledge that someone she truly cared for was actually in love with her was remarkable. Their kisses deepened and the passion Trina allowed herself to feel began to roar through her body.

Trina pulled away from her and took Rosalie by the hand. "Come with me," she said.

They hurried off the porch and walked at the edge of the garden. The swing on the other side of the yard was away from the light the kitchen had been providing. They sat down in the swing and began kissing again. Trina loved the way Rosalie immediately reached for her breasts, her hand quick to claim what she wanted. Rosalie's touch became breathtakingly slow as she further explored under Trina's shirt.

"Should we be doing this here?" Rosalie whispered. She tilted her head back so Trina could kiss more of her throat.

"Better here than on the porch," Trina said. "Or in the garden." Excitement began to rush through her all over again. "Or in the grass with the fire ants," she mumbled as Rosalie got Trina's bra undone just before taking a firm nipple into her mouth.

Pants were unzipped while the kissing continued. Trina was determined to get past Rosalie's silk panties and slip her fingers inside of her. They worked together to find a more comfortable position in the swing, then Rosalie opened her legs allowing Trina to continue what she had started. Rosalie was deliciously wet as Trina began a slow, delicate stroking. Rosalie's deep sighs and heavy breathing were easily bringing Trina right along with her.

Like an appetizer before the entrée, Trina's efforts were stimulating and produced results much too quickly. Trina loved the way Rosalie wilted against her afterward and covered her face with tiny kisses in appreciation. Trina felt as though she couldn't get close enough to her, so she kept her fingers inside of her and kissed Rosalie's forehead as she held her with her other arm.

"Now what about you," Rosalie said in a dreamy, far-away voice. She moved just enough to be able to kiss Trina on the lips. "Ask me to spend the night."

Trina smiled and retrieved her fingers from between Rosalie's legs. "Would you please spend the night?"

"I'd love to."

The double bed in Trina's room was small and noisy, so they piled quilts and blankets on the floor and made a cozy place in the middle of the room.

"Just turning over in my sleep at night makes it sound like I'm having an orgy in here," Trina said as she tossed two pillows onto the pallet. She smiled as she watched Rosalie, wearing nothing but the T-shirt Trina had given her, smooth out wrinkles on the top quilt.

"They seemed happy that I was staying over," Rosalie said.

Trina set the alarm clock down on the floor next to them. "They like you." Turning off the lamp by the bed, Trina carefully found the pallet in the dark and lay down next to her. "Aunt Reba told me earlier that you were good for me."

"She's right, you know," Rosalie said.

After removing all of their clothing, Trina adjusted the sheet they were under and then took Rosalie in her arms.

"Now elaborate on this aversion you have to my apartment," Rosalie said.

"I still can't believe I told you about that."

"Well, you did, so out with it. What have you imagined went on there?"

"Imagined?" Trina said. "Where did you and Arty do it? His work truck?"

"I'm not going to answer that question."

Trina kissed the top of Rosalie's head. She didn't want to argue anymore. She considered it a tiny miracle that she had Rosalie back again. "You don't have to," Trina said. "I already know where things took place. In your apartment and in that bed you sleep in every night."

"More of that reliable LaRue gossip?" They both laughed. Rosalie said, "Let me ask you this. How many women have you slept with in your Dallas apartment? In that same bed you and I have shared?"

"That's not the same."

"It's exactly the same."

"None of those women were related to you." Trina reminded herself not to get upset. As if Rosalie were reading her mind, she kissed Trina's upper chest and rested her hand on her stomach.

"I can't argue that point," Rosalie said. "Now let me get this right. It doesn't matter to you that possibly other men might have also been to my apartment and could have shared my bed. It just matters that Arty might have."

"I can't believe we're having this conversation," Trina said. "We're alone and we're naked and we're talking about you and your old boyfriends?"

"You're the one who made this an issue."

"Not while we were naked."

Rosalie giggled. "Well, that's true." She kissed Trina on the cheek. "I have a few suggestions on how we can work through some of this. Let me say what I have to say and then we can sleep on it and talk about it more tomorrow. Is that a deal?"

"After you stop talking, I want to make love again."

"That was understood already," Rosalie said.

"So what suggestions do you have?"

"I think we should move in together. Find a bigger place . . . a place that's ours." Rosalie kissed Trina's cheek again and then continued. "I think we should both get rid of our bedroom furniture and shop for something with less baggage and no history. A king-sized bed big enough to accommodate our active imaginations."

That struck Trina as amusing. She gave Rosalie another hug and a kiss on top of the head. "But I love my bedroom furniture."

"I love mine too, but that's not the issue," Rosalie said. "It's just furniture and it's keeping you away from me. I think it should all go and we'll just start over again with something new."

"It sounds silly when you put it that way," Trina admitted. "You're right. It's just furniture."

"It's not silly if it's causing us problems." Rosalie moved her hand from Trina's stomach to her chin. She tilted Trina's head toward her and kissed her gently on the lips. "It's your turn now, baby. I want to make you sleepy Rosalie's way."

Trina closed her eyes and let her. Eventually they fell asleep in each other's arms.

Trina spent her first day on the new job getting to know her employees and learning her way around the hotel. Roscoe Hobart and his assistant Dee Cockran were helpful and were readily available throughout the day. Rosalie was due there any minute. Trina wanted to have her office in a more orderly fashion before she arrived.

One of her first things to have to deal with as the new Food and Beverage Manager was the stack of guest complaints about slow room service. Trina would have to put in several extra hours checking to see what the problem was in the kitchen. It was obvious from the dates on the complaints that this was a fairly new problem. She wanted to get it resolved right away.

Trina's telephone rang on her desk. She answered it and smiled when she heard Rosalie's voice.

"I'm coming into the lobby. Where are you?"

"I'll be right there," Trina said. "Stay where you are."

Trina liked how Rosalie was interested in her new job and her thoughts on everything. Trina had never had a lover be so focused on her in this way. It was new and unexpectedly fun. When Trina saw her in the lobby, she was struck by how young and elegant Rosalie looked. Not wanting to drive across town for a change of clothes this morning, they found something from Aunt Reba's closet for her to wear. Rosalie had on a pair of Aunt Reba's black cotton slacks and a white oxford shirt with a black string tie that Juanito had loaned her that morning. The most interesting thing about Rosalie's borrowed outfit was the way she was able to look so feminine in clothes that should have the complete opposite affect.

"What a beautiful lobby," Rosalie said.

Trina led the way back to her office near the hotel lounge. As soon as they were inside and had the door closed, Trina took Rosalie in her arms and kissed her.

When they finally broke away from each other, Trina said, "My first kiss in my new office."

Rosalie gave her a playful swat. "It better be!" She turned around and gave the room a good look. "Is this comparable to the office you had in Dallas? You never took me there."

"We were busy doing other things whenever you were in Dallas, remember?" Trina reminded her. "It's about the same. Only in my old office I had a window."

Rosalie turned around. "Have you had time to think about anything we discussed last night?"

Trina nodded. "I have."

"And? Are you ready for us to move in together?"

"I've never lived with a lover before," Trina said. Uncomfortable about being honest, she expected to break out in a sweat at any minute.

"Neither have I," Rosalie said. "I was with my family for eighteen years and then I had roommates in a dorm in college. But that's not the same."

"What if I'm not very good at it?"

Rosalie shrugged. "We'll never know until we try. We could give it three months or so and see how we do. Or we can each get places of our own and see how that works out."

Trina smiled. "So you're really considering moving out of the love den?"

"I'll be ready to look for a new apartment tomorrow after work. It's up to you whether I get my own place or we get one together." Rosalie smiled. "I don't mean to put any pressure on you." She came over to her and kissed Trina lightly on the lips. "I just don't want to live anywhere that makes you uncomfortable, so I need to relocate soon. I can't spend many more nights on that floor in your old bedroom at your Aunt Reba's house."

Trina didn't know what to say. Once again, Rosalie had done the impossible. She had made Trina feel loved and wanted.

"The food really is good here," Rosalie said as she took another bite of her chicken enchiladas.

They were dining in the hotel restaurant. Officially Trina was off work for the day, but she still liked keeping tabs on what was going on there.

"Is it okay with Reba and Juanito if I stay with you again tonight?" Rosalie asked.

"Of course it's okay."

"Will you call them and ask them please?"

Trina smiled. "You're really something, you know that?" she said, picking up her cell phone and dialing Reba's number. When Juanito answered the phone, Trina said, "Rosalie wants to know if she can come over and play with me again tonight." Trina held the phone away from her ear so Rosalie could hear Juanito's hearty laughter. Rosalie turned a bright shade of red and made an audible groaning sound.

"So I can tell her yes?" Trina said into the phone. "Very

well. Then we'll see you later." She pushed a button and set the phone back down on the table. "It's fine with them," Trina said and took a bite of her taco salad.

"I'll do my own calling next time," Rosalie said. "There's one more thing I want to discuss with you. It has to do with Arty."

Trina stopped chewing. She disliked the way she felt whenever she heard her brother's name.

"I think it would be a good idea for the two of us to see him and tell him about our relationship," Rosalie said. "It'll give you a firm idea about how things are between Arty and me and it'll also bring my relationship with you out in the open with your family."

"That part of my family doesn't care anything about me or what I do," Trina said. "I also have no intention of seeing my brother about anything."

"It's just a suggestion, Trina. I'm still a little blown away that you think I'll go back to him some day. Arty and I are not on the best of terms."

"I have no desire to spend any time with my brother," Trina said. "Send him a letter or leave a message for him at the shop if you think it's important."

Rosalie smiled. "Better yet, why not let Reba start the ball rolling with the LaRue gossip machine?"

Trina chuckled at the thought. "She never talks to them about me, but I could plant a suggestion for you if you'd like."

"I just want you to feel better about all of this," Rosalie said. "That's important to me."

Trina felt that familiar lump forming in her throat. Seeing Rosalie trying so hard to please her made Trina want to do the same for her in return. For the first time in several years she was ready to inch out on a limb for someone.

"Do you need to stop by your place and get some clothes for tomorrow?" Trina asked. "Or are you willing to take your chances with Aunt Reba's closet again in the morning?"

Rosalie laughed. "I'll stop on the way and pick up something from my place."

"Can I go with you?"

Rosalie looked at her and Trina watched as her lovely face softened. "Sure you can."

Trina was glad Rosalie let it go at that with no questions and no assumptions. Trina was finally ready to give this relationship everything she had.

Chapter Thirteen

Trina expected to feel a lot different in Rosalie's apartment than she did once she arrived there. She could see Rosalie everywhere she looked, from the Hummel figurine collection in the maple display case to the Nancy Drew and Dr. Seuss books lined up in a bookcase. With several small antique tables helping to accent certain areas of the living room, the apartment was just as neat and orderly as Trina thought it would be. The roses Trina had sent her were sitting prominently on a glass coffee table and well on their way to opening. Trina identified with them immediately, seeing herself very much like a tight rosebud attempting to relax enough to finally enjoy being a rose. While looking at the vase, Trina realized that neither she nor the roses had reached their full potential yet.

As she checked out the entertainment center that filled the majority of one wall, Trina noticed Rosalie's impressive collection of Disney movies and several Robert Cray CDs. After a moment she mustered the courage to follow Rosalie into the bedroom where she found her rummaging in the closet. Trina sat on the edge of the infamous bed and slowly ran her hand over the pale blue comforter.

"It's just furniture," Trina said.

Rosalie lowered the dress she was holding and smiled at her. "You're being so brave sitting there."

Trina laughed, glad she didn't feel as jealous as she thought she would. By making a conscious effort to try and overcome this obsession she had with Arty, Trina hoped to stay out of therapy. She had promised herself she would seek counseling again if her feelings about Arty didn't improve. She had come a long way over the years and had no desire to jeopardize this new relationship.

"You think it's brave of me to be sitting on this big bad bed?" Trina asked. "Bravery has nothing to do with it. I just stopped being an asshole for a few minutes." She patted a place beside her. "Come here."

Rosalie hung the dress back up in the closet and went to sit next to her. Trina put her arm around her waist.

"What's it like having me here?" Trina asked.

"It feels nice and at the same time it makes me nervous," Rosalie admitted.

"Why does it make you nervous?"

"Because I know how hard this has to be for you." She lay her head on Trina's shoulder. "Anytime we face our fears it's something to be proud of."

"It's silly to be afraid of a bed," Trina said quietly. "Like you said, it's just furniture."

"This isn't about furniture, Trina. This is about trust and feeling safe. I want you to feel safe here. Emotionally safe. I

111

want you to feel that way no matter where we are." She raised her head and kissed Trina on the lips.

"Why do you care about that so much?" Trina asked. She loved the way Rosalie urged her down on the bed before leaning over her and kissing her again.

"I care because I love you," Rosalie said.

She seemed to touch Trina's breast without thinking about it, something she did automatically whenever they were laying in this kind of position.

"You know," Rosalie said as she moved a wisp of hair away from Trina's brow, "there are times when I feel as though I love you beyond all reason. I took a tremendous chance with all of this. I came out to my parents the same day I broke the engagement to Arty. I never once looked back and I gambled on having the love and support of my family."

"What made you do such a thing?" Trina asked. With a smile, she added, "What could you have possibly been thinking?"

Rosalie pursed her lips. "The way I felt about you is what made me have to do it. Above all else, I needed to be true to myself. This is who I am and those who care about me will have to accept certain things."

"You probably told your parents in a much more delicate fashion than I told mine at seventeen."

Rosalie's hand was now under Trina's shirt, slowly circling her right nipple through her bra. She leaned over and kissed Trina again. Before Trina realized what was happening they were pulling off their clothes.

"That's how much I love you," Rosalie whispered in a raspy, lust-filled voice. "Beyond all reason . . . without shame or regret . . . with complete and utter devotion."

Trina was rolled onto her back with Rosalie on top of her wildly kissing her neck and throat. *She loves me*, Trina thought. *She really does love me.* She buried her face in Rosalie's sweet-smelling hair and continued the kissing frenzy

Rosalie had started. As their hot, pulsating bodies merged and carried them forward into orgasmic bliss, Trina wanted nothing more than to hold her trembling lover and listen to her labored breathing once they were finally still again.

"Guess what?" Trina said. She touched the soft fleshy part of Rosalie's ear with the tip of her tongue and whispered, "This is a great bed. Let's keep it."

Even though Trina moved her clothes and a few personal items into Rosalie's apartment, they continued to have dinner with Aunt Reba and Juanito almost every evening. The four of them took turns cooking, or either Trina or Rosalie would pick something up on the way over after work. Trina wanted to let her aunt know she wasn't just around when she needed something. She and Rosalie truly liked Reba and Juanito's company.

It was a Kentucky Fried Chicken night and Trina was the last to arrive at Aunt Reba's house. Carrying the bucket of chicken and the bag of side orders, she found Rosalie and Juanito talking in the kitchen. Trina set the bucket and the bag down and kissed Rosalie on the lips.

"How was your day?" Rosalie asked.

"Uneventful for the most part," Trina said, "but I did locate the problem with the slow room service. Where's Aunt Reba?"

"She thought she spotted a squash bug," Juanito said with a wink and a nod toward the back yard.

"The vegetable section at the grocery store doesn't have bugs," Trina said. She went out on the back porch and saw Aunt Reba sprinkling powder on one of her plants. "That stuff can't be good for you either."

Reba waved and finished what she was doing. She picked up her hoe and put it away in the shed. "What's for dinner?"

"Chicken," Trina said as she held the back door open for her. "With mashed potatoes, gravy and baked beans."

"We'll all blow up for sure with a menu like that." Reba took off her floppy hat and hung it on the hook by the back door. "Kentucky Fried Chicken," she said. "Great chicken, but Juanito used some of their mashed potatoes to patch the sidewalk once, I think."

Despite the laughter in the kitchen, Trina made a mental note to not get mashed potatoes next time. They all sat down to eat and passed the chicken bucket around the table.

"I talked to a friend about retired gay and lesbian teachers attending the support group meetings," Rosalie announced. "She was delighted that you two were interested. Our next meeting is tomorrow evening if either or both of you are interested in going with me. I can stop by and pick you up on the way and drop you off afterward."

Trina was surprised and happy to see Reba's eyes light up.

"You interested, Juanito?" Reba asked.

"Actually," Rosalie said to Juanito, "there's only one other gay man who attends regularly, so he would welcome not being the only guy there."

"What's he look like?" Juanito asked.

"That's not why we're going," Reba said over everyone else's laughter.

"That's not why *you're* going," Juanito clarified.

"So you three are off to a meeting tomorrow night," Trina said. She looked at them and couldn't imagine how she had gotten so lucky. Rosalie's eyes met Trina's from across the table. Rosalie threw Trina a kiss and then smiled.

Trina worked late the next day and had dinner at the hotel's restaurant. She had discovered the day before that two of the employees working in the kitchen had been having an affair. Both were married to other people and were subsequently fooling around at work instead of tending to business. She had witnessed the flirting, innuendoes and groping, but had only heard rumors about the quick sex in the cooler while hotel patrons had been waiting for their room service orders to be prepared and delivered. Both employees had perfect work records otherwise; this seemed to be a new development. When Trina talked to them individually, they were each fearful of losing their jobs. Trina told them both what the problem was and showed them the stack of guest complaints. She took them off the same schedule and put them on opposite shifts. A few hours later she called several employees into her office and gave them each enough passes to Sea World to take their families. Trina made sure both employees she had spoken to earlier were there to receive their tickets. She didn't want to give either employee an excuse to spit in her food when she wasn't looking, and by giving tickets to her entire staff she didn't feel as though she was rewarding anyone for bad behavior. Trina would give tickets to the rest of her employees who were working other shifts when she saw them.

After dinner at the hotel, Trina drove to Rosalie's apartment. She needed to make a decision soon about whether or not to buy a house or get a condo big enough for two. Rosalie's apartment was nice, but there was no room for Trina's furniture. She still had it all in storage.

She set her briefcase down and turned on the news as soon as she got there. She wondered how Aunt Reba and Juanito were doing at the Teacher's Support Group meeting. All three of them had been so excited about attending together.

She heard a knock on the door and went to answer it, only to find her brother Arty standing there. They were both stunned to see each other, but the look on Arty's face and the number of inches that his jaw hung open was just short of comical.

"What the hell?" he finally said.

"It's nice to see you too, Arty. What are you doing here?"

"What are *you* doing here?"

She thought it wise not to tell him that she lived there, but instead asked, "What is it you want?"

"Where's Rosalie?" he demanded.

"She's not here."

"If she's not here, then why are you here?"

"That's not the question of the hour. I'll give her a message if you like."

"I'll talk to her myself," he said. "I'll just wait for her inside."

"No," Trina said, blocking the door so he couldn't come in. "I'll tell her you were here." She closed the door in his face and leaned back against it. Still unsettled by the shock of seeing him again, Trina jumped when he smacked the door once with his fist. She heard him walk away and felt emotionally drained once he had gone. She sat down on the sofa and started clicking through the channels one after another. It helped calm her down even though she didn't linger more than a few seconds on each program. Trina must have fallen asleep that way, holding the remote, because voices outside the apartment door woke her up with a start a while later. She heard a key in the door and then Rosalie's angry voice. Arty was with her as they came into the apartment together.

"They have laws against stalking, Arty," Rosalie said.

"You changed your phone number," he said. Arty's voice had a whiny tinge to it.

"You left me no choice."

Trina turned up the TV while Rosalie switched on every light in the apartment. She came over to where Trina was sitting on the sofa, anxiety and fear in her eyes.

"Are you okay?" Rosalie asked her quietly. Her voice broke and Trina wasn't sure what to do.

"I'm fine. He came by earlier."

"What's *she* doing here?" Arty asked, raising his voice, sounding more like himself again.

Feeling at a loss about what to do, Trina asked Rosalie if she wanted her to leave.

"No," Rosalie said emphatically. "You're not going anywhere." To Arty she said, "I told you to stop calling me and I asked you to stop coming over here."

"I just want to talk to you," he said. "Give me five minutes."

"What's the point, Arty? It's over."

"Five minutes."

"You've already had your five minutes," Rosalie said. "The last time you were here and the time before that."

"Then give me five *more* minutes!"

Trina stared at the TV and kept the sound turned up in hopes she and the neighbors wouldn't hear what was being said.

"Five more minutes won't make any difference," Rosalie said. "It's over, Arty. I'm in love with someone else."

"What!" Arty shouted. "You're what?"

"You heard me."

"Who? No way! No way!"

Trina heard the door open and then heard Rosalie ask him to leave.

"I'm not leaving until you talk to me!"

Trina heard the door close again.

"Lower your voice and sit down," Rosalie said.

After a moment Trina realized the yelling had stopped. Afraid to turn and see what they were doing, she lowered the volume on the TV.

"Trina," Rosalie called from across the room. "Come over here, please."

Trina switched the television off and then stood up. When she turned around she saw Rosalie and Arty sitting on opposite sides of the dining table.

"What?" Trina asked.

"I'm about to tell him who I'm in love with."

Frozen in place, Trina said, "That's not a good idea."

"It's way overdue," Rosalie said, "and he has the right to know."

"Can I have a word with you in private first?" Trina asked. Torn between wanting to be somewhere else if this was going to happen and at the same time not wanting to leave Rosalie alone with Arty, Trina wasn't sure what she should do.

"Excuse us for a minute, Arty," Rosalie said as if she were being rude to a guest.

Trina followed her into the kitchen where they immediately began whispering.

"You can't tell him," Trina said.

"He'll find out sooner or later."

"What if he makes trouble for you at school?"

"He won't," Rosalie said. "He knows better."

"He's a *jerk*! Arty isn't going to take this news well."

"I don't expect him to," Rosalie said, "but I've owed him an explanation for what happened and why I had to cancel the wedding."

"What did you tell him before?" Trina asked.

"I just said that I couldn't marry him. I think that's part of the reason he's not giving up and why he kept calling me." Rosalie looked at her and smiled. "Thank you for not being angry that he's here."

"It's not your fault that he's here, but I'm worried about what he might do. What if he goes to your boss or makes trouble for you at school? That won't be a pleasant thing, Rosalie."

"I'm not worried about it. Besides, I think my boss is a lesbian, too."

"Really? Since when?"

"None of that matters anyway. I have the Indian on my side."

"Indian? What Indian?"

Rosalie seemed to be ready to get things moving. She motioned for Trina to follow her back into the dining room. "Let me do the talking."

118

Chapter Fourteen

Trina watched the exchange between Rosalie and Arty, taking some pleasure in seeing Arty's eyes widen and his face change color several times. He was still in his uniform and must have stopped by on his way home from work. Trina also surmised that Arty had stomped away earlier only to await Rosalie's arrival somewhere in the parking area of the apartment complex. During Rosalie's explanation about how the wedding cancellation had come about, Arty periodically seemed to have only one thing to say.

"No way," he mumbled again for what had to have been the tenth time.

"I'm sorry I didn't tell you sooner," Rosalie said. "I wasn't sure how to go about it exactly."

Up to this point Trina thought Rosalie had done very well describing how she had come to terms with her sexuality. Everyone remained calm. It was obvious Rosalie didn't want to hurt Arty. Trina briefly allowed herself to wonder about when these two had last been intimate. Being as Rosalie had never been with a woman before, Trina wondered what could have possibly made Rosalie draw any type of conclusion about what was right for her in a sexual sense.

"Anyway," Rosalie continued, "that's basically it. I know I prefer women," she concluded. "I'm sorry I never realized any of this before you and I became so involved, and I'm sorry if the broken engagement . . . well . . . all of this was a surprise to me as well."

"Involved?" Arty said. "*Involved*? You were going to be my wife! That's a little more than involved!" He shook his head. "No way. There's no way you're a dyke."

With that said, Trina noticed the change in Rosalie's expression at the mere utterance of the word "dyke".

"Call it whatever you like," Rosalie said. "The bottom line is that I'm with Trina now."

Arty's head snapped around and he glared at his sister.

"You?" he yelled. "*You* caused this?"

"She didn't cause anything," Rosalie said, "and please lower your voice."

"What did you do to my girlfriend?" Arty was standing up now and leaning across the table toward Trina. His eyes were wide again and he had a small dab of spittle at the corner of his mouth. Trina moved her chair back away from him.

"Arty, please," Rosalie said. "Sit down."

"There's no way this is true," Arty said. With a thud, he plopped back down in his chair. "No fuckin' way."

"It's true," Rosalie said simply.

Arty stood up again only this time he grabbed his crotch. "You liked *this* too much!" he said, giving his package a firm shake in Rosalie's direction. "No way you're a dyke!"

Trina could see the horror in Rosalie's expression. It was

all Trina could do to keep from laughing. *He's a real prize,* she thought.

"How dare you," Rosalie seethed. "Get out."

"You're damn right," he said. Arty pointed his finger at Trina in a slow, threatening way and said, "You haven't heard the last of me, you fuckin' bitch."

"Get out," Rosalie said again. "Don't you dare threaten her or me. Do you understand what I'm saying?"

"You made a fool out of me."

"You were a fool before I ever met you," Rosalie said. "Now *get out!*" She left the table and marched to the door and yanked it open. "One more thing, Arty," Rosalie said. "If you make one teeny, tiny bit of trouble for me or for Trina, I'll tell my brother about the Indian."

Arty let out a gasp. "You wouldn't," he said, barely controlling his rage.

"Try me!" Rosalie said as she continued to hold the door open for him. "Besides, I'm sure you wouldn't want your buddies to know that you turned your fiancée into a lesbian, now would you?"

Arty stormed out the door and Rosalie closed it firmly behind him. She leaned her head against it and started to cry. Trina went to her and turned her around. She took Rosalie in her arms and kissed the side of her head.

Rosalie sniffed. "Did you see him grab his . . . his . . ."

"His Mr. Willie?" Trina finished for her.

"Oh, God," Rosalie said, chuckling through her tears. "You even know what he *calls* it!"

Trina laughed and hugged her. "He's always called it that. I think all men name their penises."

Rosalie sniffed again. "When he grabbed himself that way and said 'you like *this* too much' I wanted to reach over and cup your breasts and say 'but now I like *these* better!' "

They held each other until the laughter as well as the tears were finally under control. Still sniffing, Rosalie said, "I'm glad that's over with."

Trina put her arm around her waist as they walked toward the sofa together.

"It's not quite over with yet," Trina said. "I want to know all about this Indian."

Trina liked Rosalie's suggestion that they discuss the evening's events in bed. Once they got settled, Rosalie nestled sweetly in Trina's arms. "Sunset Station," Rosalie said as she pulled the sheet up to cover them. "Next to the Alamodome downtown. Familiar with it?"

"I work two blocks from there."

"Do you remember when the Indian on top of it was stolen several years ago?"

"Vaguely," Trina said. "Didn't they eventually find it in a warehouse someplace?"

"Guess who helped steal it off the top of the train station?"

Trina turned her head so she could see Rosalie better. "Arty? Chicken-shit Arty? Afraid of heights Arty?"

Rosalie laughed. "Yes. Chicken-shit Arty. He drove the get-away truck that they hauled it off in. He and his friends got drunk one night, climbed up there and took it down. Arty was drunk enough to think the heights factor wouldn't be a problem, but his friends soon discovered he was more trouble than he was worth. They ended up suggesting he stay on the ground and work the ropes from below. He was bragging about it one night after a few beers." She kissed Trina's cheek. "Arty forgot that my brother is a police officer. I have names, dates, a description of how they did it and where they kept it once the statue was down. I imagine the charges wouldn't be any more than criminal mischief or some benign misdemeanor at the most, but Arty is scared of the police."

Trina laughed and hugged her. She loved having Rosalie naked in her arms this way. "You're right. He is," Trina agreed. "Authority figures have always kind of freaked him out. He even drives the speed limit, ever notice that? It's also the reason he did everything you said tonight. When you get that 'Teacher Projection' thing going in your voice, he's at your mercy." In her best Rosalie imitation, Trina said huskily, "Arty, sit down! Lower your voice. Arty, get out. Quit grabbing your crotch!"

Rosalie's laughter made Trina laugh also. She felt safe and happy and kissed the top of her head as she hugged her closer.

"Okay, so maybe you have Arty in line with the Indian threat," Trina said. "Let's hope he stays that way."

"He will. Just the thought of his friends being in trouble because of him telling me about it is more than enough to keep him quiet."

"You're a devious woman," Trina said with a chuckle. "Now tell me what happened at the gay teacher's meeting tonight. How did Aunt Reba and Juanito do?"

"You should have seen those two," Rosalie said. "Juanito and Ron hit it off right away, which was good, and Reba spent the evening sharing gardening tips with two women I had never met before. She had a small group around her each time I looked for her." Rosalie nestled deeper into Trina's arms. "Oh! Juanito had a great suggestion that got everyone excited and might be a major project for the group in the future."

"Really? What was the suggestion?"

"That we help sponsor a gay and lesbian prom for high school kids. We would find another local gay/lesbian organization that's more out than we are, but we'd do some fundraising and behind-the-scenes work. We have several school districts in San Antonio and gay and lesbian kids from all over the city could attend."

"Juanito has talked about that for years," Trina said with a chuckle. "It really made him an advocate when he knew how many gay kids there were in my high school who wouldn't go to the school prom."

"Well, he made his pitch and got the group all fired up," Rosalie said. "They formed a committee to look into it for next spring, so needless to say, Juanito and Reba were welcomed with enthusiasm. They did fine and they had fun. As a matter of fact, Reba volunteered to host the next meeting."

Trina kissed the top of Rosalie's blond head again. "Thank you for taking care of them this way."

"Those two don't need help from anyone."

"You know what I mean."

"Yes, I know what you mean," Rosalie said. Trina could tell from the sound of her voice that she was getting sleepy. "Oh, they also were interested in some kind of bus trip to Louisiana for a weekend of gambling. An overnight thing someone had a flyer for. There was also another one to Laredo for shopping across the border. Juanito offered his services as an interpreter and a bargaining tool. I'm telling you those two were in fine form."

Trina was nervous about meeting Rosalie's parents and making a good first impression. She finally decided they would either like her or they wouldn't. She didn't know much about them other than that they were also teachers, and had liked Arty. Trina reserved judgment, and hoped they would do the same. She knew it would take more than one dinner together in order for the Cofaxes to form a well-rounded opinion of her, but it was still important and Trina wanted to make the best of the situation.

She met Rosalie back at the apartment after work early Friday evening. Trina already knew what she wanted to wear when she came out of the shower.

"Where did your parents go to school?" Trina asked.

With an amusing smile, Rosalie gave her a rundown on where her parents had gone to college. "It's going to be fine, you know."

Trina thought she was doing well until Rosalie said that. She looked at her black pants and gold, silk shirt laying on the bed and suddenly decided maybe a skirt and jacket would be a better choice. She put the slacks back in her part of the closet and selected something else to wear.

"What are you doing?" Rosalie asked as she put on an earring.

"Something less dykey, perhaps."

"Let me pick something out for you," Rosalie suggested.

Trina was surprised at the relief she felt. She slipped into panties and a bra and went back into the bathroom to dry her hair. When she came out she saw the black pants and the gold, silk blouse laying on the bed again. Rosalie was dressed and ready, sitting on the edge of the bed.

"Trust me, lover," Rosalie said as she eyed her with appreciation. "There's nothing dykey about you no matter what you're wearing. You'll be fine."

Trina carried the bottle of wine when they got out of the car. The Cofax house was in a nice neighborhood in a subdivision north of San Antonio on the other side of the airport. Rosalie explained that when she was a kid they practically lived in the country, but now there were so many new subdivisions opening up north of the city, her childhood home and the neighborhood she grew up in didn't even look like the same place anymore.

"We used to have deer in our yard," Rosalie said as they came up the sidewalk. "My brother and I would feed them corn every day and while we were sleeping at night the deer would eat whatever new plants my father had set out in the yard over the weekend." With barely more than a light knock, Rosalie opened the door and called out to her parents. Trina wondered if they had been checking her out through the drapes in the living room.

Rosalie introduced everyone.

"It smells wonderful in here," Trina said.

Rosalie sniffed. "Is that crockpot pot roast we smell?"

"Indeed, it is," Mrs. Cofax said.

Rosalie hugged them both as if it had been weeks instead of days since she had seen them. Trina couldn't remember the last time her parents had hugged her. She had no idea why that thought had entered her mind. Things like that never popped in her head anymore.

"The asparagus is steaming and the broccoli is in the microwave," Mrs. Cofax said.

Trina could see quite clearly what Rosalie would look like in another twenty-five years. Alicia Cofax was an attractive woman and her daughter looked just like her. Rosalie did, however, have her father's startling blue eyes and his blond hair.

"What can I get you ladies to drink?" Peter Cofax asked.

Rosalie leaned closer to Trina and whispered, "Would a glass of wine help?"

Trina smiled. "I'm fine."

"We'll have something caffeine-free," Rosalie said. "Whatever you have in the house."

Trina followed Rosalie into the living room and went directly to the pictures on the mantel over the fireplace. There was a picture of Rosalie's brother in his police uniform and one of Rosalie in a cap and gown taken when she graduated from college. There was also a photo of the four Cofaxes that seemed recent.

"I've been told that dinner will be ready shortly," Peter said as he handed them their drinks. "I understand that you work at one of the Regal Palace Hotels," he said to Trina.

"That's right. I've just recently transferred here from Dallas."

"How long have you worked for them?" he asked.

"Going on six years now," Trina said. "If you need a place to hold a banquet or a dinner for a family reunion or something of that nature, please give me a call. I can get you a good deal."

"Oh, really?" he said, perking up a little. "We always have a staff party at the end of each school year and we're usually looking for a nice place to have it." He nodded his approval. "That's very good to know. Thank you."

"We have one also," Rosalie said. "What kind of deal could we get?"

Rosalie's smile made Trina all warm inside. "For you I could arrange an open bar happy hour at cost and a nice selection of hors d'oeuvres, compliments of the house." She turned to Peter Cofax and said, "And, of course, the same arrangements for any celebration you or your wife would want to have there as well. In the event that food is more of a priority, then something along those lines can be worked out also."

Peter nodded again. "*Very* good to know."

Alicia called to her husband from the kitchen and he went to see what she wanted. Once they were alone, Rosalie tilted her head and studied Trina for a moment.

"How much do you know about plumbing and leaky faucets?" she asked Trina with a smile. Rosalie slowly moistened her lips with the tip of her tongue. "I was just wondering how much of that you picked up as a youngster."

Trina was surprised by the question, but certainly liked the way it had been asked. "I happen to know a lot about leaky pipes and faucets, as a matter of fact."

"Then I have a job for you the next time we're here," Rosalie said. "The bathroom in one of the guest rooms upstairs has a bad leak."

"So then it's true," Trina said, meeting Rosalie's teasing gaze. "You're really just marrying me for my plumbing . . ." she said, hesitating for just a moment before adding the word, "skills."

PART II

TRINA

Eight Months Later

Chapter Fifteen

It was a good day for barbecue so Trina and Rosalie stopped and picked it up on the way to Reba and Juanito's house. Trina's car smelled like brisket and sausage, and out of the corner of her eye she could see Rosalie balancing a pecan pie on two huge bags filled with tightly wrapped savory meat and a variety of side orders.

"So after lunch we're going shopping with them?" Rosalie asked.

"Not *shopping* shopping," Trina said, remembering how animated Reba had been earlier. She smiled and shook her head. "That part wasn't made very clear, but I think we're going with them to check out some kind of furniture place they've found recently."

It was the Saturday after Thanksgiving and Trina's first day off in over a week. All hotels downtown were filled to capacity and she had been very busy in preparation for the holiday. Reba had called earlier to tell them about the latest garage sale adventure she and Juanito had been on that morning.

"We received a job offer!" Reba had said excitedly. She explained how, over the last few weekends, they had been running into the same person at many of the yard sales they had gone to. "After seeing what was for sale at each house, we'd all get in our own vehicles and drive to the next address on our list."

Trina could so easily picture everything Reba had described to her. As a teenager, Trina had gone with them "garage sailing", as her aunt called it, only one time. The hours had not been conducive to those of a teenager back then. Trina had preferred sleeping late on Saturday and Sunday mornings.

"Finally," Reba continued, "after we met up with this woman again at three more yard sales today, we laughed and waved at each other every time we got to a new location. So as Juanito and I were looking around and seeing what was available at the last yard sale, this woman came up to us and said, 'Why don't I just give you a list of what I'm looking for so I can sleep in on the weekends?' " Reba laughed heartily into the phone. "She sounded just like you! That's something you would have said!"

Trina enjoyed her Aunt Reba's enthusiasm, but it was never made clear what exactly happened with the other person. So, since everyone was tired of eating turkey already, Trina made arrangements for her and Rosalie to bring lunch over and spend the afternoon with them.

She parked her car in the driveway and took the pecan pie from Rosalie.

"So you're not sure what we're all doing later either?" Rosalie asked.

"Not really," Trina said, "but she asked if we'd go with them this afternoon and she never does anything like that."

"I know. That's why I'm so curious," Rosalie said. "I'm also eager to find out what they've been up to recently."

Trina was still amazed as the four of them got in her car after lunch. Reba and Juanito were in the back seat while Rosalie was in the front and in charge of giving directions. Trina had an idea about where they were going, but Rosalie had been officially put in charge of navigation. Trina kept peeking in her rearview mirror and enjoyed seeing Reba in action in the back seat, talking non-stop. Trina couldn't remember the last time she had seen her so excited. Juanito was more reserved, but he also liked the proposition they had been offered earlier in the day.

Trina pulled into the parking lot of the Antique Villa and noticed right away that the lines for the parking spaces were a nice shade of lavender. There were also purple pansies in the huge wooden barrels on both sides of the front door and more purple pansies along the walkway. They all laughed when Juanito pointed to the beautiful little perennials and said, "If I were a flower, that would be me. A purple pansy."

Trina winked at him and said, "Well, you're not purple yet, but you've always been a pansy."

The door jingled as he opened it for them. Trina liked the place as soon as she went in.

"Cricket!" Rosalie said. "What a surprise to see you! What are you doing here?"

"Are you working?" Aunt Reba asked.

Cricket came around the shiny wooden counter to give

them each a hug. Reba and Juanito also knew Cricket from the Teacher's Support Group meetings they had been attending.

"Two of my best friends own this place," Cricket said. "I'm just helping out while Marcel is away in Paris for a while."

"Cricket Lomax," Rosalie said, "I'd like for you to meet my partner, Trina LaRue."

"I've heard so much about you," Cricket said. "It's nice to finally meet you."

Before Trina could say anything, Cricket started showing them the newest antiques they had recently gotten in. There were two other customers there looking at a roll-top desk in the corner.

"Oh, honey," Reba said. "We're not here to shop. We're here to see Ms. Morales."

"Carmen?" Cricket said. "She's in the back. I'll get her for you."

Cricket opened a door and disappeared for a few minutes and then came back. "She'll be right with you." Lowering her voice she said, "How am I doing? I get nervous when a lot of people are here and they start asking me antique questions."

Juanito smiled and said, "Now by 'antique questions', do you mean *old* questions, or do you mean questions about antiques?"

"Only someone who *was* an antique would ask me such a question, sir," Cricket said. They both laughed and she hugged him again. Trina could tell that Juanito liked to tease her. Had either of them been straight, their interaction might have been referred to as flirting.

Trina made her way over to the corner where the two other customers had been. They were now looking at an oak table on the other side of the room. Trina ran the palm of her hand over the roll-top desk and could easily see it in her office at home.

"Isn't this beautiful?" Rosalie said as she came up alongside her. She reached over and read the $450 price tag and showed it to Trina. Rosalie smiled. "I already know what you're thinking."

Trina glanced over at her and met Rosalie's tantalizing expression. "You do?"

"Yes, I do," Rosalie said. She nodded toward the desk. "You're thinking about how nice this would look in your office at home, aren't you?"

Trina leaned closer and whispered just loud enough for Rosalie to hear, "I was actually thinking about how nice this desk would look if you were sitting in the middle of it naked."

Rosalie's eyes flew open. The squeak that came out of her mouth made Trina chuckle.

"You, my love," Trina whispered, "would make any piece of furniture absolutely priceless with nothing more than that visual in mind."

"You made it," came a voice from the doorway leading to another area of the store.

"Yes, we did," Aunt Reba said as she whirled around. "Let me introduce you to my niece and her partner."

Trina liked Carmen Morales's firm handshake, and also noticed how bubbly Aunt Reba became around her. Trina assumed Carmen was a lesbian not only from her neat, starched appearance, but also by the way she carried herself. She had short black hair peppered with silver highlights, and a nice sincere smile. Reba, Juanito and Trina followed her to the back of the store to a work area. Rosalie and Cricket stayed behind, deep in conversation with the other two customers.

"This is where I do all the refinishing and any repairs that are needed," Carmen said. "I'd like to tell you what I have in mind and you two let me know if it's something you'd be interested in."

As Carmen spoke, Trina and Juanito walked around the

work area in the immediate vicinity where Carmen was talking. Trina saw several large pieces of furniture in various stages of refinishing. There was a huge fan drawing out air and another one circulating the air inside. The fumes from furniture strippers and other refurbishing products wasn't as offensive as Trina expected. There was sawdust on the floor near where an impressive table saw was located.

"I would like for both of you to be watching for antique furniture that's for sale at these places you go to," Carmen said. "We're looking for anything that's made of wood. If it's not damaged or missing pieces, then that's even better. If it's a nice piece but needs a few repairs done to it, that's also doable."

"What kind of furniture?" Juanito asked. "Just anything made of wood?"

Carmen nodded. "Basically, yes. Tables, desks, old bed frames, dressers, book cases."

Trina couldn't help but smile as she watched Aunt Reba listen to every word. *She's smitten,* Trina thought. *How cute! I've never seen her this way before!*

"My business partner usually acquires our inventory, but she has a family emergency and will be out of the country for a while," Carmen said. "I've been trying to do both the buying as well as running the shop. The only time I'm able to really work on the furniture is on the weekends when Cricket is here to help out front and then in the evenings after the place closes. So it would be very helpful to me if you two could keep an eye out for any antiques at the yard sales you're going to."

Trina could see Juanito had noticed Aunt Reba's infatuation with Carmen. He had his hands clasped behind his back, suppressing a grin as he looked over at Trina.

"Before we continue," Carmen said, "is any of this something you two are even interested in doing?"

"Oh, yes," Reba said before Juanito could even open his mouth. "We're very interested."

136

"Good," Carmen said, looking obviously relieved. "Then let me tell you what I have in mind."

Trina listened to Carmen's offer. Reba and Juanito were being given a large amount of responsibility. Carmen was letting them use a truck on the weekends as well as during the week, if they were also interested in going to estate sales as well.

"I would need a receipt for anything you purchased," Carmen said, "and you would be reimbursed for whatever amount you paid for each furniture piece."

"What if we buy something you don't like?" Juanito asked. "Or something you can't fix?"

"If it's made of wood, I can fix it," Carmen said with confidence.

"Oh," he said with a laugh. "Then what if we find something that's really big?" Juanito pointed toward a wardrobe that was at least seven feet tall.

Carmen walked over to the wardrobe and fondly touched its side. "I can make arrangements to have it picked up later in the day, but you'll need to have paid for it already."

"I have a question for you," Trina said to Aunt Reba. "How is this new responsibility going to affect your regular 'garage sailing' activities?"

"It won't affect it at all," Reba said with a furrowed brow. "Like Carmen said, we would be there anyway, so we might as well look for furniture while we're out."

Trina looked over at Juanito and raised her eyebrows. He nodded, so Trina kept quiet and let them do what they needed to do.

"Any other questions?" Carmen asked.

"No," Juanito said. "I think we've got it."

Carmen threw her head back and laughed. "You haven't even asked about what's in this for you and all your trouble!"

"What do you mean?" Reba asked.

"I don't expect you to do this for free," Carmen said. "I

was thinking that fifteen percent of the purchase price for each piece would be fair. Our markup is outrageous, so we'll just tack that on to the resale price."

Trina noticed that Juanito perked up with the mention of the fifteen percent offer.

"Then why don't we try this out for a few weeks and let's see how we do," Juanito suggested.

Carmen handed over the keys to the truck that was parked outside in the back. Trina followed them out there and was impressed. The truck looked new and had a lift on the back. Carmen showed Juanito how to use it and then explained how the magnetically-attached logo for the Antique Villa on both of the truck's doors needed to be removed. Carmen took them off and set the logos behind the seat in the truck.

"If you leave these on," Carmen said, "the sellers tend to jack up their prices. I only put them on the truck when I'm delivering large furniture pieces or out doing errands."

"Then after we're finished for the day," Aunt Reba said, "we just drop off what we've found?"

"Yes," Carmen said. "Then I'll write you a check for everything that day and add the commission. It's very important that you remember to get a receipt." She smiled and shrugged. "It's also a tax thing. Any other questions?"

"I don't have any," Reba said.

"Sounds easy enough to me too," Juanito said as he put the key to the truck in his pocket.

Trina followed them back into the workshop area and wondered why this woman was so trusting. *She doesn't even know these two*, Trina thought. *They can be trusted with anything, but how does this Carmen woman know that?*

They went back through the other door and into the show room where Rosalie, Cricket and the other two customers were. Cricket was ringing up a sale. Trina felt a pang of disappointment when Rosalie told her someone had just bought the roll-top desk.

"*My* desk?" Trina said as she searched for it across the room in the corner. "So I'll never get to see you —"

"I'm afraid not!" Rosalie said with a delighted laugh.

Chapter Sixteen

All the way back to Reba and Juanito's house, Juanito relentlessly teased Reba about mooning over Carmen.

"You were ga-ga, Ms. Thang," Juanito said.

"I was not!"

"You should have seen her this morning," he said as he reached over the seat and tapped Rosalie on the shoulder. "We arrived at the first yard sale early, as usual, and I was helping the guy drag all the stuff out. Carmen pulled up and asked if they had any furniture for sale. He said yes, so she started helping us get everything out of the garage. Carmen buys a small beat-up table and a headboard, pays cash for them and then she's ready to go. Now all of a sudden guess who *else* was ready to go? Did I get a chance to dig for the pocket knife the guy promised me was in a junk box labeled 'Everything Here $1 Each'? Nooo! Reba's dragging me to the car by the ear and we're suddenly following Carmen's truck!"

Trina enjoyed hearing Rosalie's laughter and Aunt Reba's blanket denials about how the events that morning had actually unfolded, but Juanito was far from finished.

"Then once we're in the car," he continued, "she says to me 'Speed up. You're going to lose her!' and then when I'd speed up she'd shout, 'Slow down! She's going to see us!' "

By now all four of them were laughing.

"Okay, okay," Reba said finally. "So maybe there's a grain of truth to his story, but at no time was I *ever* mooning," she added.

"Yes, you were!" the other three said at the same time, which made them laugh all over again.

"Who wants pie?" Juanito asked as soon as he got the front door open.

Trina followed everyone into the kitchen and then joined Aunt Reba at the table. Trina wondered what she was thinking. Reba was quiet and pensive, and even though she had handled their earlier teasing well, she now was keeping her thoughts to herself.

"I know that look," Trina said to her. Juanito was busy making coffee while Rosalie was getting plates and forks out for the pie.

"What look?" Aunt Reba asked.

"Tell me what's on your mind," Trina said. "I can see the wheels turning from here."

Reba shrugged and took the knife that Rosalie handed to her to cut the pecan pie with.

"Carmen needs help during the week," Reba said. "You heard her say that the woman who usually works out front is away on a family emergency."

"And?" Trina said.

Reba took a deep breath as she slid generously-cut slices of pie onto the plates. "I think it would be a nice thing if I were to maybe volunteer my services to help out there during the week."

Whoa, Trina thought. *She's been retired for three years and never has had the urge to work anywhere other than in her garden!* Trina glanced around to see if Juanito or Rosalie were paying attention. She caught the grin on Juanito's face, and Rosalie looking intently at Reba.

"Yes, that would be a very nice thing to do," Trina said. "But are you sure you want to give up so much of your free time that way?"

"Squash bugs," Juanito reminded her with a smile.

"I could call Cricket right now and see what she thinks of the idea," Rosalie offered.

Everyone seemed to have suddenly shifted gears and were no longer teasing Aunt Reba about her infatuation with Carmen. They had become a low-profile cheering section.

Reba's eyes lit up. "It's too late in the year to grow squash and here's the phone number for the Antique Villa," she said as she pulled a business card out of her shirt pocket. "We'll wait."

"Carmen wants to talk to you," Rosalie said. She handed over the phone to Reba, then returned to the table where Trina and Juanito were already sitting.

Trina smiled as she watched Aunt Reba smooth away imaginary wrinkles on her clothing before saying anything. Trina leaned closer to Juanito and whispered, "Look how nervous she is."

"There's something I forgot about," Rosalie said. "Remind me to tell all of you when she gets off the phone."

Trina tried to listen to her Aunt Reba's end of the conversation. The other two were doing the same. Juanito poured them all coffee, while Rosalie set napkins under each person's fork. By the time Reba was off the phone, the table was immaculate and pie was the last thing on anyone's mind.

"Well?" Trina asked. "What did she say?"

Reba was absolutely glowing. "She was so excited about my idea! She must've thanked me at least ten times."

"When do you start?" Juanito asked.

"I'm to go in tomorrow at nine and work with Cricket all day," Reba said. "She'll show me what to do, then I'm on my own as of Monday. But Carmen will be there Monday. She'll be in the back working on other furniture."

"You're okay with these arrangements?" Trina teased her. Trina did not envy any person who tried to keep Aunt Reba *away* from the Antique Villa now.

"Oh, yes," Reba said. "Carmen insists on paying me, but I need to check with Cricket to see if she's getting paid. I'm offering my services as a volunteer. I don't need the money."

"It might be more work than you think," Rosalie said. "See how adamant Carmen is when you discuss it with her tomorrow."

They finally began eating their pie, then Juanito reminded Rosalie that she had something to tell them.

"Oh!" Rosalie said. "I remember talking to Naomi once about Cricket and her lover. Apparently the woman who owns the Antique Villa with Carmen is someone named Marcel. She and Carmen were in the Army together. When they retired they opened the antique store. Marcel and Cricket have been best friends since they were children. It just so happens Cricket and Marcel's mother are lovers. They've been together about two years now. Anyway, Marcel is French and still has relatives in Paris."

"Wait a minute," Juanito said. "She's French, but she was in *our* Army?"

"Yes," Rosalie said. "West Point graduate, too. Retired as a Colonel, from what I remember hearing."

"Wow," Juanito said, obviously impressed. "Was Carmen an officer, too?"

"I don't know about that," Rosalie said. "My brother was in the Army for three years, that's the only reason I asked Naomi any questions about it at all when we were talking."

"What else do you know about these women?" Trina asked.

"Naomi and Marcel are lovers," Rosalie said. "Naomi and Cricket trade off working weekends at the Antique Villa to help Carmen out. Apparently Marcel's grandfather in Paris is very ill and she and her mother go back there quite often."

"What else do you know about Carmen?" Aunt Reba asked.

Trina couldn't help but laugh and enjoyed seeing Reba blush again.

Rosalie smiled and met Reba's inquiring eyes. "I've only met her one other time. She was over at Naomi's one evening measuring her bedroom so they could deliver new furniture." She looked over at Trina. "It was that weekend last spring when you were being such a jerk."

To Trina's surprise all three of them roared. "When was I a jerk?" Trina asked.

"When? Or which time?" Reba said, which again made everyone but Trina laugh.

"You know when," Rosalie said. "Our first big argument. Where you didn't call me for two days."

"You didn't call me either!"

"Anyway," Rosalie said, pretending to ignore her. "Carmen and Cricket were at Naomi's house when I got there that night. The four of us sat around and discussed the problem I was having with my girlfriend."

Trina set her fork down and suddenly remembered Carmen's comment earlier in the day. When she, Juanito,

Aunt Reba and Carmen left the workshop area and went back to the show room where Rosalie and Cricket were, Carmen shook Rosalie's hand and said, "We've met before." Rosalie then introduced Trina as her partner and Carmen looked at Rosalie with a smile and then asked, "Is this *the* girlfriend?" Rosalie had chuckled before saying yes.

"So you had already discussed my jerkdom with a total stranger?" Trina asked. She was having a problem finding anything funny about this, but the other three were still rolling with laughter.

Rosalie finally got up out of her chair and came around behind Trina and put her arms around her neck. She kissed her just below her left ear and said, "You're not really a jerk all that often, babe, and when you are — you're *my* little jerk."

That endearing declaration seemed to make things better and eventually, even Trina laughed.

Trina was having trouble making time to do any Christmas shopping. It was very busy at work and tourists from up north were everywhere in the stores downtown where it was more convenient to shop. She did manage to make a room reservation at her hotel for the same night that Rosalie's staff Christmas party was scheduled. Trina was also glad Rosalie's parents had taken her up on the offer to also hold their staff Christmas parties at Trina's hotel. In addition, the Gay and Lesbian Teacher's Support Group had made arrangements for their party at Trina's hotel. She had made a reservation for her and Rosalie that night also.

One evening in mid-December, on a rare occasion when she and Rosalie were dining at home alone together, Rosalie asked Trina how they would be spending their first Christmas.

"Christmas Eve is usually when my family gets together," Rosalie said. "That would leave us available to spend Christmas Day with Reba and Juanito."

"You and I can get up early and open our presents," Trina said with a grin. *I have got to do some shopping this week*, she thought.

"My mother plans to call Reba and invite them over for Christmas Eve also," Rosalie said as she set out a salad.

Trina had been setting the table and looked at her. It was hard for her to believe how nice Rosalie's parents were. Even after knowing them for nine months, and being made to feel like a part of their family from the first day, Trina still found herself waiting for the proverbial "other shoe to drop." So far, that hadn't happened, and now this? That Aunt Reba and Juanito were to also be a part of the Cofax family holiday celebration? It was almost too much to comprehend.

"They would really do that?" Trina asked.

Rosalie looked up at her, momentarily confused. "Of course they would."

Trina's eyes clouded over with unexpected tears. The next thing she knew, Rosalie was putting her arms around her.

"What's the matter, baby?" Rosalie whispered.

"I don't know," Trina said as she buried her face into Rosalie's sweet-smelling neck and hair. She couldn't vocalize her feelings. She didn't know how to tell her what it meant to have Rosalie in her life and to be part of a family again . . . or how much it meant to be accepted by people she respected and cared about . . . people who also respected and cared about her in return. Trina couldn't speak. All she could do was hold onto Rosalie tightly to thank her for all the love she had given her.

"Your parents are very nice people," Trina finally said with a sniff.

Rosalie kissed the side of Trina's head. "You're a nice person too, and so are Reba and Juanito."

When they finally let go of each other, Trina could see that Rosalie also had tears in her eyes.

"After dinner let's go get a Christmas tree," Rosalie said.

Trina felt the love spreading through her heart as she finished setting the table, and wondered again how she had gotten so lucky.

Chapter Seventeen

Trina managed to get the last of her Christmas shopping done on what should have been her lunch hour. She had wrapping paper all over her desk and gifts piled up under it. She had to remember to keep her office locked; every three minutes or so there was some sort of problem calling her away.

It was December 18th and Peter Cofax's staff Christmas party was due to begin within the hour. Trina had given her own staff explicit instructions about how she needed the evening to go.

"Keep the hot wings, chips and salsa, cheese sticks, and fried mushrooms coming all night," she told her waitstaff. "No empty plates or bowls. Don't hover, but be there when they need something."

Trina would also be helping behind the bar to speed service along and to keep an eye on how things were going. These were her "in-laws"; she wanted everything to be perfect.

Two nights later, Alicia Cofax had *her* staff Christmas party there. The first one, for Peter's coworkers, had been a booming success and both of her "in-laws" had recovered enough already to enjoy this party as well. Again, Trina helped behind the bar and made sure the hors d'oeuvres kept coming and the party-goers were happy. There were also three other parties going on in different conference rooms in the hotel. Trina would check in on all of them off and on during the course of the evening. By the end of the night she was exhausted.

Then came the night of the Gay and Lesbian Teacher's Support Group party. Again, there were four Christmas parties going on at the same time and again, Trina had to keep an eye on each one. Rosalie arrived with Juanito. Aunt Reba was coming to the party with Carmen. For weeks now, Trina had spent a total of three hours on the phone with Aunt Reba trying to reassure her it was okay to ask Carmen to go with her to the party.

"She already knows people there," Trina told her earlier in the week. "I say go for it!"

After that conversation, Trina had gotten Aunt Reba's excited call the following day at work. Carmen had happily accepted the invitation and had volunteered to pick Reba up and take her. So with a little romance in the air to add to the regular holiday festivities, it was a busy and exciting time. At least now Trina had something else to watch for other than how many drinks certain patrons had consumed during the evening. According to Texas Law, the establishment serving liquor was responsible for the condition of each customer it served. Trina hoped that designated drivers had already been appointed, but just in case that hadn't been done, she had made arrangements to have several taxis out front anyway.

Trina was behind the bar when she saw Cricket and a nice-looking older woman arrive. Cricket waved and the two of them made their way over to the bar.

"Everything is decorated so pretty!" Cricket said. "Good job, Trina."

"Thanks. Can I get you two something to drink?"

Cricket ordered two white wines and then introduced the woman she was with. "Trina, this is my lover, Roslin Robicheaux. Now Trina. Tell the truth. Isn't she hot?"

Trina laughed, not sure how to respond to that. Roslin just shook her head and turned a flattering shade of pink.

"Trina is Rosalie's lover," Cricket explained to Roslin. "You met her the other night at the meeting."

"Ah," Roslin said. "The young one." She laughed suddenly and then added, "Well, at my age they're all young ones."

Trina saw Naomi arrive with someone, and Cricket waved them over as well.

"Trina, have you met Marcel?" Cricket asked. "Marcel Robicheaux, this is Trina LaRue. She's Reba's niece."

Marcel smiled engagingly and nodded. She was an attractive woman, and Trina noticed Naomi couldn't keep her eyes off of her. *Now I remember,* Trina thought. *These are the two who have been away in Paris.*

"Your Aunt Reba has been a tremendous help while I've been away," Marcel said.

"She's enjoyed helping out," Trina said. "What can I get everyone to drink?"

They were a lively bunch and Trina was very proud of her staff for keeping a good attitude and a sense of humor throughout the evening. They were undoubtedly as tired as Trina was. The week before Christmas was always a back-breaking, busy time. They wouldn't even get a few days to recover after Christmas, because by then they would be gearing up for New Year's Eve as well as the Alamo Bowl football game between Iowa and Texas Tech. None of this was news to Trina's staff, however. They were ready and eager to make extra money from tips, overtime, and overall tourist generosity. But as Trina made drinks and kept the hors d'oeuvres steadily moving, she could feel the strain of being on her feet for seven days in a row taking its toll on her shoulders and her lower back.

"You look so tired, babe," Rosalie said as she came over to the bar to get refills on her and Juanito's grapefruit juice.

"How's Aunt Reba doing with Carmen?" Trina asked.

Rosalie laughed. "Did you know that until this week when Reba asked her out, Carmen thought Reba and Juanito were married? As in husband and wife?"

Trina's eyes popped open. "Are you serious?"

"They're all having a good laugh over that one," Rosalie said. "It's actually going very well. Carmen is waiting on her, making sure the salsa and chips stay close and full, and Reba's glass hasn't been empty all evening."

"Wow," Trina said. She wasn't sure she knew enough about this Carmen Morales person — other than being a nice-looking butch, was retired military, and could fix anything made of wood, there was nothing else on Trina's radar screen.

"Will you find out as much as you can about her?" Trina asked Rosalie. She continued making drinks and taking money as if she were being operated by remote control.

"Find out things about Carmen?" Rosalie asked. "Are you worried about this blossoming romance?"

Trina shrugged as she poured a jigger of tequila into a silver shaker. "Aunt Reba is falling for her. I don't want to see her hurt." She looked at Rosalie and realized what she had just asked her to do. *These are Rosalie's friends. She shouldn't have to quiz them.* "It's okay," Trina said. "I'll find Naomi later and take care of it."

Rosalie smiled and picked up the two glasses of juice that Trina had refilled. "I'll see what I can find out for you."

From there the evening seemed to fly by, even though Trina had to deal with the Food and Beverage manager at the Regal Palace River Center across the street from them. They had run out of rum and tequila and needed to borrow some immediately. Not wanting to leave her own lounge short for the evening, she made arrangements with the F & B manager at the Regal Palace by the airport to deliver extra rum and tequila to her. The three F & B managers would sort out who owed who what during the up-coming week at some point.

As the parties at the hotel started winding down for the evening, Trina and her staff started serving complimentary coffee to the guests. Texas Law also prohibited the sale of alcohol after two a. m., so she let her bartenders go home and had already arranged for the breakfast crew to come in early and help housekeeping get things back in order. Trina had a good budget for overtime during the holidays and if she could keep her staff healthy and free from colds and flu, then things would work out fine and they could all earn some extra money.

Juanito had been one of the first to leave and came over to give her a hug. He wasn't much of a drinker, so she didn't have to worry about him doing anything more than falling asleep on the way home. "Excellent party," he said as he hugged her. "I need the recipe for those hot wings."

"They come in a box already seasoned," Trina said. "Can't help you there."

A while later as Trina was scraping chicken bones into a trash can, her Aunt Reba came over to say good-night.

"She *insisted* on taking me home," Reba whispered in Trina's ear.

"To your home or her home?" Trina asked, only half teasing.

Reba threw her head back and laughed. "*My* home, silly!"

"Just checkin'." Seeing how happy her Aunt was, Trina

gave her an extra hug and wished her luck. "How much has Carmen had to drink?"

"Two drinks early in the evening," Reba said, "then Diet Coke the rest of the time."

"Okay. I'll call you tomorrow," Trina said. "I want a full report." She watched as Aunt Reba went back to the table; Carmen put her hand on Reba's back and escorted her out of the lounge. They occasionally stopped along the way to say good-night to their friends.

Naomi and Cricket came over later to thank her for an excellent party. Cricket was more bubbly than usual, but had a cup of coffee in her hand.

"Tell me you're not driving," Trina said to Cricket.

"Me?" Cricket said with a snort. "Oh, heavens no! Marcel will get us all home."

"Okay. I'm glad everyone had a good time."

"We had an *excellent* time," Naomi said. "We'd also like to book another party in March. I'll ask Rosalie to get with you on that next week."

Much later as Trina was making her rounds at the other parties in various stages of wrapping up in the Bowie Room, the Travis Room and the Crockett Room, she walked in on a man and woman in the Travis Room about thirty seconds away from intercourse behind the sound equipment that hadn't been dismantled yet. She recognized the man as the DJ she had seen earlier in the evening, but had no idea who the woman was. The flash of a penis was one of the last things she wanted to ever see, and instructed him to break down his equipment — stopping long enough to add "stereo equipment" — and to get things out of there as quickly as possible.

Trina was then paged to the lounge for a phone call. Who could be calling her at this hour? The Regal Palace River Center couldn't possibly need anything else from them. They should also be attempting to get ready for a seriously busy breakfast run soon.

"Trina LaRue," she said into the phone. She waved at Rosalie who was across the room still talking to Naomi and Marcel. Trina could also see Cricket sitting down at a table with her head on her lover's shoulder.

"It's Juanito," he said. "I know you're busy, but I had to call you."

"No problem. What's up?"

"Your Aunt Reba and Carmen are parked in the driveway. They've been there for about five minutes making out like teenagers!" His laughter was just short of a giggle.

"What?" Trina said. She couldn't help but laugh, too. "Where are you?"

"I'm in the living room peeking through the drapes. Where do you think? I'm not missing this!" He chuckled again. "I wonder if she's got her shirt off yet?"

"Damn! What else can you see?"

"Not much," Juanito said, "but enough to know what's going on. Another five minutes and they'll have the car too steamed up to see anything!"

By the time Trina got up to the hotel room she had reserved weeks ago, Rosalie was already asleep. Trina had told the front desk she didn't want to be disturbed for anything unless it was an emergency. When she finally got her clothes off and crawled into bed, a sleepy Rosalie put her arm around Trina's waist and asked what time it was.

"Four-thirty."

"You poor baby," Rosalie said. She kissed Trina gently on the lips. "You must be exhausted."

Trina was too tired to even answer.

"Everyone said they had a good time tonight." Rosalie turned over on her back and pulled Trina into her arms.

"I'm glad."

"I talked to Naomi and Marcel about Carmen," Rosalie said with a yawn. That managed to perk Trina up a little.

"What's the verdict?" Trina asked. "Is it okay if Aunt Reba wants Carmen to come out and play?"

Rosalie laughed and kissed the top of Trina's head. "She's a good catch, from what I hear. Thirty years in the Army. Does carpentry and wood-working as a hobby. She's the co-owner of a successful business, owns her own home, has a big family here in town who embraces her lifestyle, never been married and hasn't had a lover in over ten years. She even sounds sane and stable."

"Then why is she single?" Trina asked sleepily. "Aren't wackos the only single ones left these days?"

"You used to be single," Rosalie reminded her.

"Maybe we shouldn't go there," Trina said as she kissed her on the cheek and chuckled. "In the morning remind me to tell you about Aunt Reba and Carmen making out in the driveway tonight."

"What?" Rosalie said, giving Trina a shake. "Wake up. That can't wait until morning." Glancing over at the clock she said, "Besides, it's already morning."

Chapter Eighteen

On Christmas Eve, Trina was still wrapping gifts in her office. She'd already given her staff their presents as well as the desk clerks, Roscoe Hobart and his secretary, Dee Cockran. Now all she had to do was wrap Juanito's and two more for Rosalie.

She had finally gotten a full night's sleep the night before, but felt she could easily catch another twelve hours and not even move. The hotel was still filled to capacity, but the guests there now were more mellow on Christmas Eve than they would be for the rest of the holidays. Trina predicted the following week would be the worst, with rowdy college football players and their fired-up families and out of state fans. Trina and her staff would once again be working long hours and teetering on the brink of exhaustion by the time the new year arrived. She was just glad Rosalie was off work for the holidays and had volunteered to do the rest of the Christmas shopping for them. Trina had been put in charge of finding something for Juanito and, of course, her own gifts for Rosalie. Each year Trina promised herself she would start shopping earlier, but things just never seemed to work out that way.

As she finished wrapping the last three gifts, her foot hit something under her desk. She moved her chair back and saw four more presents underneath. Trina sighed heavily. *You still have those to wrap*, she thought. The paper and bows for the remaining gifts were also stashed under her desk, and Trina knew it had been a good idea to keep them out of sight these last few days. She usually became depressed once it got closer to the time she would visit her parents and her brother, but Trina vowed to get it over with as quickly as possible the next day. This was the time of year she always felt closer to her Aunt Reba and Juanito. They loved her no matter who she slept with. She also wanted to make her first Christmas with Rosalie in their new home a memorable one. In a way, she liked thinking of Christmas Day as their anniversary.

Peter Cofax had gone with a Peanuts theme for his Christmas decorations. He had a huge stuffed Snoopy asleep on top of a dog house and several flood lights placed in the yard that were accenting other wooden Peanuts characters holding song books for caroling. In addition, the massive oak tree in the front yard was decorated with tiny white twinkling lights. The house, sidewalk, and driveway had red and green lights outlining everything. Trina could tell that a lot of work had gone into it.

"Merry Christmas!" Peter yelled from the doorway as Trina and Rosalie got out of the car.

Trina reached for the bag of presents in the back seat and threw it over her shoulder with a jolly, "Ho, ho, ho." When she got to the door with it she handed the bag to Peter and said, "*Oy vey.* That's heavy."

Rosalie's brother Wesley pulled up and parked behind Trina's car with his own load of presents to bring in.

"Merry Christmas," Wesley said to Trina, giving Rosalie and his mother a hug. "It's supposed to get colder tonight."

Before they could get the front door closed, Juanito and Reba drove up.

"Oh, good," Alicia Cofax said. "We're all here."

"I'll go see if they need any help," Wesley said.

"They're supposed to be bringing some of the tamales we made," Rosalie said. "What a job *that* was!"

Trina smiled at her. That's all Rosalie had been able to talk about for the last two days: Tamale-Making With Juanito Gomez.

"They're still commenting on how nice the Christmas party was at the Regal Palace," Peter said to Trina. "How far in advance should we be making reservations if we want the same arrangement for next year?"

"Tamales!" Wesley said as he came in carrying two huge shopping bags for Reba. "I can smell them through the foil."

"Where's Lois?" Alicia asked her son. "I thought she was coming with you."

"We sort of broke up last week, Mom," Wesley announced.

"Oh, goodness!" she said. "I'm sorry to hear that. What happened?"

Wesley looked at his mother. Obviously, he couldn't believe she asked him such a thing in front of so many people. Rosalie laughed and slapped her brother on the back and said, "Yeah, Wes. Tell us all about what's going on in your personal life before we even have our first cup of eggnog."

"I'm sorry," a chastised Alicia said. "You're right. It's none of our business."

"Things just weren't working out," Wesley said to his mother. He then turned around and announced to everyone else, "In case anyone in the other room missed that, I said things just weren't working out!"

Juanito waved and acknowledged they had all heard him just fine.

"Well, you could have mentioned something before now," Alicia said.

Trina watched with amusement as Rosalie slapped her brother on the back again and said, "Yeah, Wes. You could have said something sooner. Trina and I get dibs on Lois's presents. By the way, does she even know you two have broken up yet?"

"She knows."

"You don't seem too upset about it," Rosalie said with a touch of seriousness in her voice.

"It was a mutual decision," Wesley said. "She's now dating a friend of mine so all's well. Who wants eggnog? It's ready, right, Mom?"

"It's ready," Alicia said.

Earlier Rosalie had also been talking about how good her mother's eggnog was, describing it as a vanilla shake with a kick. Trina tried some and liked it, making it her drink of choice for the first half of the evening.

Trina decided to go easy on the eggnog once she got a nice buzz. After noticing the volume of laughter in the Cofax's living room, Trina also realized she wasn't the only one enjoying that particular beverage. In the corner Trina could see Aunt Reba and Peter Cofax discussing gardening plans for the spring and the possibility of installing small greenhouses in their back yards so they could garden all year round. Trina was surprised when Alicia came over and asked her to help with setting out the food. Rosalie seemed to be too busy relaying her tamale-making experience to her brother to notice anything else happening in the room.

As Alicia unwrapped the first dozen tamales and put them in the microwave to heat up, she said, "Rosalie is so proud of these tamales. Next time Juanito makes them, Peter and I would like to help. She made it sound like so much fun."

"It is fun," Trina said, "but it's also a lot of work." Taking a deep breath and closing her eyes to the wonderful smell of steamed corn shucks and a myriad of spices, Trina said, "For me this is what Christmas smells like. It's the only time Juanito makes them." She smiled and took the foil off another dozen tamales and put them on a paper plate to be warmed next. "I wanted to thank you and Peter for opening your home to Aunt Reba and Juanito tonight. It's meant a lot to me and to them as well."

"They have made Rosalie feel like a member of their family," Alicia said, "and we already feel as though we have two daughters now." She leaned closer and gave Trina an impulsive hug. "Having all of you here is what Christmas is about for us."

Trina swallowed in hopes of keeping the lump in her throat from growing. Rosalie was like her mother in so many ways. It was easy for Trina to visualize her lover in twenty years.

After they got everything ready, Trina went back into the living room to tell the others that the food was now being served. When Trina got there she couldn't help but notice how close Wesley was standing to Juanito. They were by the fireplace with Rosalie, holding their cups of eggnog and talking. Wesley's body language was relaxed and less macho than she had ever seen him. *Maybe it's the eggnog*, she thought. *Or maybe Juanito is telling one of his many stories about teaching. He definitely has a way with a story.*

"I'm ready to sample those tamales," Peter said.

"You should see the size of the pot we used to cook them

in," Rosalie said as everyone began making their way to the dining room. "I kept thinking that some hot tubs weren't even that big."

In the hallway, Juanito sidled up alongside Trina and whispered, "These are delightful people and they sincerely care about you. I hope you're aware of that."

"I am," Trina said, feeling warm and happy hearing someone else confirm what she herself already knew. "What's your impression of Wesley, by the way?" Trina whispered.

Juanito gave her a wicked grin. "He's a curious young man."

"I see. Tell me more." *Curious?* Trina thought. *Hmmm. Interesting word choice there, Juanito.*

"My gaydar let off a beep or two," Juanito whispered, "but he's also a cop. He could be setting me up for something. I've always been of the opinion that a wise man never plays with a police officer no matter how tempting his little handcuffs and night stick are." His laughter made Trina laugh also.

"What's so funny over there?" Rosalie called from the dining room.

"Mr. Gomez is trying to get me in trouble," Trina said. "No more eggnog for him."

Even as the evening began to wind down, the volume of laughter in the Cofax's living room never seemed to get any lower. Trina loved listening to what she was beginning to think of as "the sounds of Christmas." She already had the smell of tamales to associate with the holiday, and now there was an audio perception making a lasting impression on her. She could hear a Karen Carpenter CD over the happy chatter in the living room, and the sound of bows being torn from presents and scotch tape being pulled away on a box. Trina liked scanning the sea of colors from the wrapping paper that had been strewn around the room. She also liked the way

Rosalie and Wesley stuck their bows from their presents in their mother's hair. The two siblings had extra gifts from their parents. It still amazed Trina to see how well Rosalie got along with her brother. There were times when Trina regretted not being closer to Arty now, but those were fleeting moments. Too much damage had been done over the years. He was lost forever.

"Does anyone want coffee?" Alicia asked over the constant chatter and laughter. "I've also got cake and cookies to set out."

Hands were raised for a coffee count and all four women ended up in the kitchen together to help with dessert. Alicia still had three bows stuck in her hair and seemed oblivious to them.

"Did you see the new blue sweater I got?" Rosalie asked Trina. They were setting out the cookies in the dining room with Rosalie arranging them nicely on a plate.

Trina smiled. The Eggnog-Rosalie was very animated. Trina had an overwhelming urge to kiss her and tell her how happy she was, but instead she said, "Yes, I saw your new sweater. It's going to look lovely on you. It matches your eyes."

Rosalie put more cookies on another plate. "So what kind of presents do I have at home under the tree?"

"What kind?" Trina asked. "You have Christmas presents at home under the tree."

"I know that!"

Trina laughed again. *Yes, indeed,* she thought. *Eggnog-Rosalie is very cute and very hot.*

"Coffee should be ready in a minute," Aunt Reba said as she came out of the kitchen and into the dining room. "Leaded and unleaded are brewing as we speak. So what time are you two coming over to the house tomorrow?"

"I imagine we'll be sleeping in," Trina said, raising her eyebrows and nodding toward Eggnog-Rosalie.

Reba laughed. "About one then?"

"We should be able to make that," Trina said. "I also have an errand to run tomorrow."

Reba looked at her and gave her a solemn nod.

"What errand?" Rosalie asked.

"Okay," Alicia said as she came out of the kitchen. "How's it going in here?"

Trina sighed, momentarily grateful for the interruption. Deep, hearty male laughter came from the living room. All four of the women turned and looked in that direction. Then Trina heard Aunt Reba's laughter and looked in time to see her remove one of the dangling bows from Alicia's hair. Trina watched her aunt hand over the bow and suggest to Alicia that she anchor it better.

"Where did that come from?" Alicia asked. She patted her hair and found the two other bows stuck there. "You kids," she said. "I forgot you two always do that to me. One year they almost let me wear one to church for Christmas Eve services."

"We've done it for twenty-five years and she never remembers," Rosalie said. She hugged her mother and helped her remove all of the sticky bows. "Let's go check on the coffee."

Trina watched Rosalie and Alicia walk back into the kitchen together. She felt the lump returning to her throat once more. Tomorrow she would see her own mother again.

Chapter Nineteen

Trina woke up Christmas morning and took just a few minutes to watch Rosalie sleep. *She might not be feeling very well today,* Trina thought with a grin. Rosalie had been cuddly and giggly the night before, laying her head on Trina's shoulder during the drive home. *I need to get that eggnog recipe from Alicia just to see what's in it,* Trina thought. She had never seen Rosalie quite that relaxed and animated before.

She propped herself up on an elbow and leaned over to whisper, "It's Christmas morning, sleepy head."

Trina heard a little groan, but Rosalie didn't offer any other type of promising movement. Trina slipped out of bed and went to make some coffee. After plugging in the lights for the Christmas tree, she took a shower. Trina contemplated letting Rosalie sleep while she went to deliver the four presents to her parents' house, but didn't like the idea of Rosalie waking up while she was gone.

When Trina came out of the bathroom after her shower, she was still drying her hair with a fluffy towel when she heard another groan come from the lump under the covers in the bed.

"What time is it?" Rosalie asked in a sleepy croak.

Trina chuckled again and glanced at the clock on the night stand as she continued to rub her hair dry with the towel. "Nine-thirty."

"My head feels like it's Christmas morning," Rosalie mumbled. "Why do I drink that stuff every year? Why, why, why?"

"Here's your water and two aspirin," Trina said gently.

"Oh, thank you." Rosalie attempted to sit up while Trina gave her the antidote. "I want a good-morning kiss," Rosalie muttered, "but I would need to brush my teeth first." She gingerly eased back down against her pillow. "I'm just not up to brushing anything right now. I'm sorry."

Sitting on the edge of the bed, Trina said, "Why don't you rest a few minutes until the aspirin begins to work?"

"Okay," Rosalie said without needing any further encouragement. She hadn't even opened up her eyes all the way yet. "It won't take long. I promise."

Trina leaned over and kissed her on the forehead. "Coffee's made and in the carafe already," she whispered. "I have to run an errand. I'll be back soon."

"An errand?" Rosalie said. Her eyes were still closed. "It's Christmas. What kind of errand? Everything's closed today."

"Go back to sleep," Trina said. "We'll open our presents when you feel better."

"Kiss me first," Rosalie mumbled. "You can't leave until

you kiss me. I've changed my mind about needing to brush my teeth."

Trina smiled and kissed her at the corner of her mouth. "You have the cutest eggnog breath," she whispered. "I'll be back in a little while."

Rosalie was asleep again before Trina even got up off the bed. Trina went to the bathroom in the guest room to blow-dry her hair so she wouldn't wake up Rosalie again. Wearing blue jeans that fit her perfectly and a pair of Roper cowboy boots that she saved just for this occasion, Trina then slipped on her NOBODY KNOWS I'M A LESBIAN T-shirt and a light jacket. Going for a butch flair even though the outfit was foreign to her, she felt certain her parents thought she dressed this way all the time. Rubbing their noses in her lifestyle once a year was one of the few pleasures she got from seeing them these days, but what was worrying her the most this time was how this annual trek didn't seem to be making her feel any better this year. Something had changed and Trina wasn't sure what had caused it.

On the drive over to her parents' house Trina cleared her mind of everything but being with her family again. She wanted to just show up, go in, pass out the presents and let them do what they needed to do in order to make their own point.

She could feel her heart pounding as she turned down their street . . . the same street she had played in as a child. The Gallaghers' home was for sale on the corner. She wondered if everything was all right with the old couple. The Gallaghers always gave out the best candy on Halloween. All the kids in the neighborhood had liked them. Trina never heard any news about her old neighbors. The LaRue family gossip only covered information gathered about individual family members.

Trina slowed down as she got closer to her parents' driveway. Her father's work truck was there and Arty's pickup was parked behind it.

"Everyone's here," she said and then took a deep breath to steady her nerves. She glanced at her watch. *Pam,* she thought. *Don't forget her name is Pam.*

Trina got out of the car and took off her jacket even though it was chilly. She wanted to make sure everyone inside could see what was written on her T-shirt. She opened the trunk of the car to get the presents out; Trina had placed them in a nice, strong bag the day before. She closed the trunk and then walked to the front door.

They've repainted the house, she thought as she rang the doorbell. *Decorations are the same as last year. Icicle lights everywhere just like all the other houses on the block have.* Trina rang the doorbell again and could finally hear some commotion going on inside. She held down the button, which made the doorbell seem louder and more spastic, and then Trina pounded on the door and yelled, "Open up! It's Christmas, goddamn it!"

Trina seldom used that type of language any time other than Christmas. Just being at her parents' house seemed to bring out the worst in her. She pounded on the door again and then it flew open, startling her.

"Merry Christmas," Trina said and elbowed her way in past her father. It was warm inside, which was in total contrast to the chilly reception she was already getting. Trina could smell a turkey cooking in the kitchen and the oranges piled high in a bowl on the coffee table. She tried to filter all of that out of her head as she announced cheerfully, "This won't take long."

By the fireplace Trina noticed a young blond woman with

a confused expression on her face. The girl looked enough like Rosalie to be her sister. Trina had to chuckle when she saw Arty step in front of her as if to keep those bad lesbian rays from zapping this girlfriend.

"You must be Pam," Trina said. "I've heard about you from other family members."

Pam didn't say anything, which didn't really surprise Trina. The only other things Trina did notice were that no one was talking to her this year and Arty seemed to have gained some weight since she had seen him last. *The night he came over to Rosalie's apartment late in the spring,* Trina thought. Her parents looked the same — her father's eyes wild with fury at her being there, and her mother wringing a starched apron as if she were somehow gaining extra strength by doing so.

"Are you okay, Arty?" Trina asked. "You look fluffier than I remember." She knelt down in front of the Christmas tree and took the four gifts out of the bag. "I've brought presents," Trina said. "Even one for you, Pam. Now don't everyone rush over here at once."

To Trina, it always seemed that her parents and Arty were usually in shock whenever they saw her on Christmas Day. They had to know to expect her. She had been visiting them this way for several years. As Trina soaked up what was happening, she noticed everything appeared to move in slow motion for the LaRues — their responses, their silence, their non-verbal insults, their inability to comprehend what was happening to them in their very own living room. As if it had been rehearsed a hundred times, Trina knew instinctively when to move back out of the way so she wouldn't get stepped on. As she did so, her father reached down, picked up his present and marched to the front door and pitched it out on the lawn. Trina watched as her mother slowly did the exact same thing as if each defiant movement were aimed directly at her. Sticking her hands in the pockets of her jeans, Trina then watched as her brother took his new girlfriend by the hand, led the way to the Christmas tree, picked up both remaining presents and then headed for the front door with them.

To Trina's amusement she heard Pam say from the foyer, "Why are we doing this?"

"Don't ask. Just do it!" Arty snapped. "Here. Gimme that!" Moments later the front door was slammed shut and they came back into the living room with Arty still holding Pam's hand.

"You know, Arty," Trina said simply, "Rosalie still has the present I gave her last year." She saw his eyes widen and his mouth fly open, but nothing came out of it. "I'm aware that you like for me to keep my visits short, so I'll be on my way," Trina said. "Merry Christmas to all of you. It's been fun, as usual."

She left them all standing there. She had to smile again as she walked by Arty and Pam. As soon as Trina got close to them, Arty put his body between his sister and his girlfriend, saving Pam from whatever it was Rosalie had contracted this very day a year ago.

Trina made a hasty exit and as soon as she was out on the sidewalk in her parents' front yard, she waved at the neighbors who were there to snatch up the four presents.

"Remind me to get in touch with you in November so I can buy something you like!" Trina called to the man and woman who lived across the street. They were holding the presents up to their ears and shaking them. It no longer upset her to see the gifts being taken away by virtual strangers. Trina could see the humor and absurdity in everyone's actions, from her family all the way down to the neighbors. *These people are all nuts and I'm the one who sought therapy?* she thought.

The neighbors smiled and waved at her as they hurried back into their yard. "Merry Christmas!" the man yelled over his shoulder when he reached his sidewalk. "Cordless drill!" he said. "That's what you can get me next year! A cordless drill!"

Trina rolled her eyes and waved at them as she got in her car.

She had trained herself for years not to get sentimental or upset by this day or whatever happened while she was with her family, but it didn't always work out the way she planned. Yet Trina had wasted all the tears she ever intended to shed over the situation. There was no reasoning with her parents, and her brother had no mind of his own. Arty would go along with whatever his father wanted. He had too much to lose to do anything other than that.

Trina watched the happy neighbors go inside their home and imagined they had spent most of the morning peering through the drapes in anticipation of her arrival. As Trina started her car, she remembered how much different things had been last year with Rosalie being the young woman at Arty's side. Trina remembered seeing Rosalie standing on the LaRues' front porch, clutching the wrapped present to her chest . . . the wrapped present she had refused to throw on the lawn. Rosalie had waved at Trina before Arty went out on the porch and reeled her back in.

After that, Trina knew Arty would probably marry her and then she would only see Rosalie once a year during her annual ten-minute visit to her parents' home on Christmas Day. Had that happened, then Trina's relationship with Rosalie would have consisted of smiles and tiny waves at funerals and then eventually pictures of LaRue grandchildren secretly placed in a Christmas card. Another thing Trina had envisioned that day last Christmas was how she would have probably seen her future nieces and nephews grow up through school pictures mailed out once a year. It also occurred to her that Arty might even expound on the twisted family tradition by throwing out Trina's presents to his own children. Coached by their father, one by one Trina could see Arty's toddlers following him to the front door just to toss a wrapped gift out on the grass. *Not all family traditions are good things,* she thought with a shake of her head.

During the drive home, Trina felt such a huge sense of relief at having that whole scene behind her for another year. Now she could celebrate the rest of the holidays the way she wanted to. Hopefully she had a warm, sleepy lover still in bed, only feeling much better by now. They still had presents to open and a late Christmas breakfast to fix together.

Trina heard the hum of a blow dryer coming from the master bathroom when she got home. She glanced at her watch and saw it was only ten-thirty. The twinkling lights on the Christmas tree made her smile. She was slowly coming back down from what she liked to refer to as the "Christmas Day Blues." Usually after she would leave her parents' house on Christmas Day, Trina would drive directly over to Aunt Reba and Juanito's house and let them nurture her back to a better state of mental health. Now she had Rosalie to come home to, and knew this was the way things were meant to be. Her life had changed for the better. Trina was happy to not carry around all those hostile emotions any longer.

"There you are," Rosalie said when Trina went into their bedroom. "Where did you go?" She looked at Trina's T-shirt and her eyes registered immediate recognition. "You went to see your parents?"

Trina pulled the T-shirt over her head and poked it in the hamper. "I need another shower after being there," she said and started taking the rest of her clothes off.

"Trina."

The tone of Rosalie's voice stopped her in the bathroom doorway.

"You went over there alone?" Rosalie asked.

Trina turned around; her feet were bare and her jeans were unzipped and hanging low on her hips.

"Of course I went alone. I always go alone."

"What was the point of going at all?"

Rosalie's questions were confusing her. Trina didn't need this now. *Nurturing*, she thought. *Where's my nurturing?*

"It's Christmas," Trina said. She stuffed her jeans and underwear in the hamper. "I need to wash off this 'Christmas with the LaRue's' feeling I always get." She went into the bathroom, which was still warm and steamy from Rosalie's shower. Trina turned on the water and tested it with her hand. After a quick rinse, she got out only to find Rosalie leaning against the bathroom door jamb.

"You're feeling better?" Trina asked as she began drying herself off.

"I can't believe you went over there today," Rosalie said. Her voice was softer now, but Trina still couldn't tell if she was angry or not.

"It's Christmas," Trina said. "I always see my parents at Christmas. You know that. We met that way, remember?"

"I remember," Rosalie said quietly. "God, how I remember." She came into the bathroom and took the towel Trina was using. Rosalie began drying Trina's back with it. "I've never been the same since meeting you that day." She kissed Trina's shoulder and then reached around to cup both of Trina's breasts. "I would have wanted to go with you this morning," Rosalie said as she continued to kiss her back, neck and shoulders. She slowly turned Trina around and lowered her mouth to one of Trina's breasts.

Just moments before Rosalie encouraged Trina to open her legs, Trina thought, *This is what I need. This is what I want. What a nice thing to come home to.*

Over and over again, Rosalie kept saying how sorry she was Trina had to go and see her parents alone. She covered

Trina's face with a string of tiny kisses, making Trina feel almost paralyzed with desire.

Rosalie led her out of the bathroom and didn't seem to care that the bed was only a few feet away from them as she urged Trina down on the bedroom floor. The cool, lush carpet against Trina's naked body felt surprisingly sensual. Rosalie was on top of her, propping herself up with her arms and searching Trina's face with so much concern and love in her eyes Trina never wanted them to move from that position.

Rosalie kissed her and Trina's body trembled. Rosalie then gently moved Trina's damp hair away from her forehead and whispered, "You'll never have to be alone with them again, baby. I promise you that." Rosalie kissed her, then asked if they had made her cry.

"Not this time."

"I'm sorry I didn't remember."

Then, as if trying to make up for her oversight, Rosalie's kisses turned into slow, lingering expressions of love and desire.

"This would be more fun on the bed," Rosalie whispered with a light chuckle.

She kissed Trina everywhere and took her sweet time making love to her. Eventually they returned to the bed where they cuddled and then continued what had started on the carpet. Rosalie made everything better with her body, her words and her heart. Trina was slowly able to put the "Christmas Day Blues" behind her in the comfort of Rosalie's arms, and move past all the hate and discontent of a family who had so easily abandoned her.

Chapter Twenty

By the time Trina woke up again they had twenty minutes to get to Aunt Reba and Juanito's house. After making love, they had fallen asleep in each other's arms.

"You'll never believe what time it is," Trina said as she threw the covers off of them and scrambled out of bed.

"How did it get to be so late?" a now wide-awake Rosalie asked. "Where did this day go?" She fell back across the bed. "We haven't even opened our presents yet!"

Trina smiled at her and then offered a hand to pull her up. "You mean there's more? That little thing you did earlier wasn't my present?"

Rosalie laughed and was now up, getting dressed. "That little thing had nothing to do with Christmas."

Trina kissed her on the lips. "We'll open our presents when we get home later. It'll give you something to look forward to." She picked up the boots she had worn earlier and set them in the back of the closet, thinking she wouldn't need them again until next year.

"I can't believe you went over there today," Rosalie said. She was buttoning up her shirt and checking herself out in the dresser mirror. "Did you have presents for them?"

"Yes," Trina said. She was nearly dressed already and gave her hair a little shake on her way to the bathroom to brush her teeth again.

Pulling on a pair of warm socks, Rosalie asked what happened. She was almost completely dressed and followed Trina into the bathroom. "How are your parents?"

After Trina finished brushing her teeth, she said, "Everything is all mixed up under the tree. I'm going to get their presents together."

"Tell me what happened when you got there."

"We'll talk in the car," Trina said. *Wow,* she thought as she went to find a bag to put Reba, Juanito and Carmen's presents in. *She has to let this go,* Trina thought. *I can't keep rehashing this all day. It's over for another year.* Trina knelt down by the tree and began sorting the gifts, making sure she got the ones she was looking for. A few minutes later, Rosalie came up behind her and kissed Trina on the side of the neck.

"That's what made us late to begin with," Trina reminded her.

"Did they throw their presents outside again?" Rosalie asked softly. Trina could hear the concern in her voice. Rosalie joined her in sorting through the gifts.

"Yes, they did," Trina replied. She smiled sadly. "Arty's new girlfriend was there. She threw hers out, too. Well, I can't

175

be sure of that. She went with him to the front door and there was a tiny discussion before Arty threw his and hers out, I think. I couldn't see exactly what happened, but all four gifts eventually ended up on the lawn." Trina stopped sorting the presents and began putting them in the bag. "She looks like you, by the way."

"Who looks like me?" Rosalie asked as she held the bag open for her.

"Pam. Arty's new girlfriend." Trina looked up at her and asked if it bothered her that Arty had a new girlfriend.

"Why would that bother me?" Rosalie asked. "It's actually a huge relief. I want Arty to be happy. I know I hurt him and that wasn't an easy thing for me to do."

"I know."

"Why did you ask me that? About whether or not it bothered me. What were you thinking?"

"I'm thinking there sure are a lot of presents here with your name on them."

Rosalie giggled and gave Trina a quick kiss on the lips. Trina tasted the minty flavor of toothpaste and kissed her back.

"I know!" Rosalie said. "And I don't have time to play with them!"

"Come on," Trina said as she got up off the floor. "Let's go. We're late."

Trina parked her car behind Carmen's truck in Reba and Juanito's driveway. She liked that Carmen was becoming a regular visitor there. Trina also enjoyed seeing the twinkle in her Aunt Reba's eyes whenever Carmen was around. She had never known her aunt to have a lover before, but then Trina had assumed all these years that Aunt Reba was just more discrete than most.

"I can't believe I slept through Christmas," Rosalie mumbled as they got out of the car.

Trina laughed. "We didn't sleep through the whole thing. It's still Christmas and will continue to be Christmas for another —" she glanced at her watch and said, "another eleven hours or so."

They both took huge bags of presents out of the back seat.

"Well, I've never in all of my entire twenty-seven years slept through a Christmas morning," Rosalie said, "and I've had plenty of eggnog headaches on this day ."

"We could have skipped the sex," Trina reminded her. She knocked on the front door and then held it open for Rosalie.

"Maybe *you* could have skipped the sex," Rosalie whispered with a laugh as they went inside.

Christmas greetings and generous holiday hugs were exchanged. Trina was amused at how Rosalie kept going on and on about "sleeping through Christmas."

"Please tell her that Christmas isn't over yet," Trina said to Juanito. "She isn't listening to me."

"So you two haven't exchanged gifts yet?" Aunt Reba asked.

"Someone didn't feel well this morning," Trina explained.

"Someone else didn't feel very well either," Juanito said. He ran his hand slowly through his hair and didn't seem to be moving around very fast. "What was in that eggnog anyway?"

"You've been in bed all this time?" Carmen asked with a smirk. Trina noticed how familiar Carmen was with things in the house and wondered how much time she was spending there. Carmen had taken Rosalie's coat and hung it up in the hall closet. She was also the one who had turned the Christmas music down when they had first arrived. Trina thought it looked quite natural to have her there. She obviously made Aunt Reba happy. That's all Trina cared about.

"I hope everyone's hungry," Juanito said.

"We slept through breakfast too," Rosalie said, following him and Carmen into the kitchen.

"You're a whiny little thing today, aren't you?" Juanito said good-naturedly as he put his arm around Rosalie's shoulder.

Just to prove him right, Rosalie said in a whiny voice, "I have a *hangover*!"

Trina leaned against the back of the sofa and watched the blinking lights on the Christmas tree. The music playing softly on the stereo, the laughter coming from the kitchen, the smell of tamales and a baked ham were all having a calming affect on her. Reba came over and took Trina's hand in hers.

"Did you see your parents this morning?" Reba asked.

"Yes."

"Things were the same?"

Trina nodded. "Not a bit different. Same scene — just another year. Everyone is looking older now and Arty has gained some weight. Other than that, nothing has changed."

"I've heard your brother has been sick lately," Reba said. She gave Trina a hug. "I've been so worried about you today, but it made me feel better knowing you had Rosalie to come home to afterward."

Trina smiled and squeezed her aunt's hand. "She was great. Well, actually, she was incredible. That's why we're late." Trina could feel herself almost glowing from the memory of Rosalie and their lovemaking earlier. She gave her Aunt Reba a fierce hug and felt at peace with herself and those she considered her real family.

"You would have been very proud of Rosalie today," Trina said. "She took it all away. She eased the bad things out of me and replaced it all with love and compassion."

"I'm proud of both of you."

* * * * *

178

It was getting dark by the time Trina and Rosalie got all their presents in the car and were on their way back home again. As Trina drove down the interstate, Rosalie set a brown paper bag in the back seat.

"I'm not sure I want to see another tamale for a while," Rosalie said. "At least not for a day or two."

Once they got home and had the car unloaded again, the festive Christmas tree in their living room seemed to capture Trina's attention.

"We still have presents to open!" Trina said.

"You get them sorted," Rosalie said excitedly, "while I go change clothes."

Trina knelt down, having done this three times already that day. This time promised to be much more fun. She made two separate piles, and liked that Rosalie had twice as many presents.

"Are we ready?" Rosalie asked from across the room. She had changed into a white terry cloth robe and had the sash snugly tied. "Look at all these presents!"

Trina had piled Rosalie's gifts on the sofa and had put her own less impressive pile on the floor beside the recliner.

"Which one should I open first?" Rosalie asked.

Trina laughed. Rosalie looked adorable sitting on the end of the sofa surrounded by presents, her blue eyes wide and twinkling, the white robe and her blond hair making her look so young. "It doesn't matter," Trina said. "I got you the same thing, but just more of it. Remember that blue sweater you got last night? I bought you eight more just like it."

"Liar!" Rosalie squealed as she ripped the paper and bow off the first present and found a pair of gold earrings. "Look at these! They're beautiful!"

Trina ended up with three very nice outfits for work, a pair of Nike Airs and a black leather jacket.

"Look at all these presents!" Rosalie said again. She still had several more to unwrap. "You're finished already?"

Trina smiled. "Some of us don't poke around where Christmas is concerned." She picked up the jacket and stood to slip it on. "This is very nice, Rosalie. Thank you."

Rosalie set one of her three remaining presents down and managed to stand up, even though she was surrounded by wrapping paper, boxes and a dozen or so gifts.

"Come with me for a minute," Rosalie said.

Trina followed her to the study where Rosalie opened the door and switched on the floor lamp in the corner.

"Carmen and her brothers delivered it for me last night while we were at my parents' house," Rosalie said. "I bought it for you the day we were at the Antique Villa."

Trina saw the beautiful roll-top desk she had admired the day they had all visited the antique shop.

"I thought those other people there bought it," Trina said. Still somewhat in shock, she went over to the desk and sat down in the new chair that went with it. Trina opened the desk drawers one at a time and couldn't stop smiling.

"You like it?" Rosalie asked.

Trina turned in the chair and held out her hand for Rosalie to come closer.

"When did you buy it?" Trina asked.

"That day we were all there," Rosalie said. "You, Reba and Juanito were in the back with Carmen, remember?"

"It's beautiful," Trina whispered. A tear rolled down her cheek, but she couldn't stop smiling.

"There's one more thing," Rosalie said. She tugged on Trina's arm and got her out of the chair. Rosalie pulled the sash on her robe, which revealed her breasts. When she crawled up on the top of the desk, Rosalie let the robe fall from her shoulders to expose her nude body.

"Remember when we were checking out this desk and I asked if you were thinking about how nice it would look here in your study?" Rosalie asked. "I think your exact words were 'I was actually thinking about how nice this desk would look if you were sitting in the middle of it naked.'"

Their eyes met and Trina felt her heart swell with love. She nodded and whispered, "Yes, I remember."

Rosalie held her hand out to her and wiggled here bare shoulder suggestively. "Merry Christmas, baby."

PART III

ROSALIE

Four Months Later

Chapter Twenty One

Rosalie got home, glad to be out of all the traffic. It was Fiesta week in San Antonio and the entire city was in the mood to party. All the hotels downtown were filled to capacity. Trina had three parties booked before, during and after the River Parade that night. Rosalie could tell Trina was tired.

"One of my new bartenders called in sick," Trina had said on the phone earlier. "I'm not sure when I'll be home. It's been such a long day already."

"Okay, baby. Then I might have dinner with Juanito and Reba. Call me on my cell phone if you need me."

Rosalie had last experienced Fiesta about two years ago when she was still dating Arty. He and his friends usually scheduled part of their vacations around that time of the year.

As an adult, Rosalie hadn't cared for Fiesta very much. Working the next day after having stayed out all night didn't appeal to her. In addition, Fiesta wasn't something her parents had ever been interested in either. There were events they attended because of specific school functions, but overall Fiesta was not something the Cofax family took part in.

While she changed out of work clothes, Rosalie called Juanito to see what they were doing for dinner. Together they decided that she would stop and pick up fried chicken on her way over.

"I'll throw a few things together here to go with it," he said. "We also have some apple pie left over from yesterday. Carmen should be here by then, too."

When Rosalie arrived, she saw Carmen's truck in the driveway already. Rosalie smiled as she got out of her car, remembering Trina's most recent comments about her Aunt Reba's sleeping arrangements.

"I bet she's staying over at Carmen's house when they do it," Trina had said.

" 'Do it'?" Rosalie repeated with a laugh. "What kind of talk is that?"

"You know what I mean!"

Rosalie disagreed. "I bet they make love anywhere they want to. They aren't kids. Why should they sneak around?"

"With Juanito in the house?" Trina said with a raised eyebrow. "Nah. Besides, he already caught them once making out in the driveway. He teased them so much they're probably paranoid about all of that now."

"I can't believe we're actually talking about this," Rosalie said. "It seems very disrespectful."

"I know," Trina agreed, "but I'm still curious. I've never seen Aunt Reba act like this before. It's kind of cute. Besides, it's not like I'm bringing it up with anyone else but you."

So, when Rosalie arrived with the fried chicken, she found Carmen and Juanito in the kitchen puttering around like an old married couple. One was cooking while the other was setting the table. Rosalie saw Reba on the phone in the corner and waved to her.

"Trina must be busy this time of year," Carmen said.

"She is."

"I'll be downtown at Night In Old San Antonio later this week working in my brother's gordita booth," Carmen said. "Anyone want to help us? I can get you in free."

"What's your brother look like?" Juanito asked. It was always his standard question. It made Rosalie and Carmen both laugh.

"He would probably knock you on your butt just for asking, *amigo*," Carmen said, still laughing.

"Then count me out," Juanito said.

"Count me out also," Rosalie added. "From what I remember about all of that, it's just a huge mob of drunk people spilling beer on each other."

Their attention shifted to Reba, who was still talking on the phone on the other side of the kitchen, but she had uncharacteristically raised her voice in anger. Rosalie, Carmen and Juanito all stopped what they were doing. Rosalie was surprised to see her slam down the receiver.

Wasting no time with politeness, Juanito asked who had been on the phone.

"My sister," Reba barked.

Rosalie went over to her and touched Reba on the arm. "Are you okay? What happened?"

"Those . . . those . . . those *imbeciles*!" Reba snapped.

"Come over here and sit down," Rosalie said. "Tell us what happened."

Carmen pulled out a chair for her while Juanito set a cold glass of grape Kool-Aid down in front of her.

"Arty is sick," Reba said. "Really sick. In the hospital type of sick."

Rosalie immediately felt alarmed. "What's wrong with him?"

"His kidneys are failing," Reba said. "He needs dialysis."

An involuntary gasp came from Rosalie as she brought her hand up to her mouth. "How is he? What hospital is he in?"

Carmen was now behind Reba massaging her shoulders; Reba seemed to almost melt at her touch.

"I knew Arty had been ill over the past few months," Reba said in a less angry tone of voice, "but no one thought we should know why until now." She pursed her lips and sighed, then reached up and put her hand on Carmen's. "Let's eat. I need to get my mind on something else before I have to deal with more phone calls later."

"Kidney failure," Rosalie said. Her mind was racing. Arty had always seemed so strong and healthy. Even though she was no longer in contact with him, Rosalie still cared about him. "How long has he been sick?" she asked.

"They don't know or they aren't saying," Reba grumbled. "But they want us all to go in for some kind of test."

"Is it something hereditary?" Rosalie asked. *Trina*, she thought, feeling alarmed all over again. *Could Trina also have inherited whatever it is?*

"Who's they?" Carmen asked. "You said *they* want you to go in for tests."

"Really," Juanito said. "They who? They family? They doctors? They who?"

"That boy's imbecile parents!" Reba said. "My homophobic turd of a brother and his homophobic turd of a wife."

Juanito raised his hands in an attempt to calm Reba down again. "You know we have a Turd Rule here in this house," he said sternly. Then with a twinkle in his eye he added, "No turd talk at the table. How many times do I have to remind you of that?"

Reba set her chicken leg down on her plate and looked across the table at him, blinking as if she had just seen him for the first time. "A Turd Rule? What Turd Rule? What the hell are you talking about?"

* * * * *

Rosalie hadn't heard Trina come to bed the night before. She turned off the alarm and got ready for work. Before she left the house she scribbled a note for her, suggesting that she call Aunt Reba as soon as she got up. Rosalie put the note on top of the toilet seat to make sure Trina would find it. At Rosalie's lunch break she called her at home.

"You barely caught me," Trina said. "I'm just leaving for work again."

"Did you find my note?" Rosalie asked. She could hear Trina's light laughter.

"Yes, I found your note."

"Did you call Reba?"

"I called Aunt Reba."

"And?"

"And it looks like Arty's very sick."

"Did Reba find out more today?"

"It also looks as though Arty will need a kidney transplant."

Rosalie felt her heart sinking. How could the rest of the family keep something this serious from them for so long? It infuriated Rosalie the way the LaRue gossip pipeline worked. Trina had several aunts, uncles and cousins who would have nothing to do with Trina or Reba because they were lesbians.

"How soon does he need a transplant?" Rosalie asked.

"He needs it now," Trina said matter-of-factly. "When I saw him in December he was already in need of dialysis. His kidneys are damaged and may not be functioning at all. There's still a lot going on that we're not being told."

Rosalie didn't trust her voice. She cleared her throat to keep from giving away her emotions.

"I'm taking Aunt Reba in for testing tomorrow," Trina said. "My parents are sending hints through the grapevine about Arty needing a donor."

"Reba made and received several calls last night," Rosalie said, "but couldn't get anyone to admit that."

"They finally did this morning," Trina said.

"So Reba's going in for testing?" Rosalie asked.

"Yes. She scheduled it this morning. If there's no match with a family member, then Arty goes on a list and waits for a kidney."

Rosalie felt a chill race up and down her arms just before a wave of nausea crept in. She rubbed her arms to get rid of the goose bumps and then took a deep breath.

"Why are you taking Reba in for these tests?" Rosalie whispered. "Why isn't Juanito taking her?"

There was a long pause . . . so long that Rosalie thought there might be something wrong with the phone.

"Trina."

Finally, Trina said, "I know you're upset about Arty's illness."

"You're having tests done too, aren't you?"

"It would be interesting to see what kind of match I would be."

"Trina." It was the only word Rosalie could say. She felt as though her throat had closed up.

"I need to get going," Trina said. "I have so much to do today. I'll call you later to see if we can have dinner together."

Rosalie couldn't even tell her good-bye. She heard the line go dead and the buzz of the dial tone echo the uncertainty that she felt.

After doing some research on the Internet, Rosalie wasn't as anxious about the prospect of Arty's kidney transplant. Rosalie had also wondered why she didn't feel comfortable showing so much emotion over Arty's illness. After work she drove over to her parents' house in hopes of speaking to her mother alone.

"I'm very sorry that Arty is sick," Alicia Cofax said. She and Rosalie were in the kitchen peeling potatoes. "I'll call the LaRues to see how they're doing."

Rosalie smiled. Just being with her mother made her feel better.

"I need to ask you something," Rosalie said, "and I'm not even sure how to do it."

"Ask away, dear."

"Trina's schedule is horrific right now. We haven't been able to spend much time together." Rosalie wasn't even sure she understood what her feelings were. "This thing with Arty has me very upset. Maybe more upset than I should be. I don't know how to talk to her about it."

"You almost married him, Rosalie. It's only natural that you wish him well. It could have been you having to deal with all of this now if you had gone through with the wedding." Alicia stopped peeling potatoes and looked at her. "You're not still in love with him, are you?"

"No," Rosalie whispered. "I'm sure I was never in love with him to begin with, but I don't want him to be sick. I want him to be happy. I want him to find a nice girl and get married. Have babies and be successful."

"He can still do all of that."

"I need for him to do it *now*!" Rosalie didn't even try to stop her tears. "I feel so guilty for screwing up his life. He loved me and I hurt him. It'll just make me feel better if he's happy and well and can go on with his life. I don't know how else to explain it."

"You had nothing to do with his current health crisis, dear. He can still find a nice girl to marry and have lots of babies. Once he gets a new kidney, everything else will work fine again." Alicia picked up another potato to peel. "You can't take the blame for everyone's misfortunes. You can't fix everything."

They finished with the potatoes and Rosalie put them on to boil.

"It's okay to be worried about Arty," Alicia continued. "There's nothing unusual about that. So what else is going on? This can't all be about Arty. What else has you upset?"

"Reba has been contacted by someone in the family about submitting to a few tests. They're looking for a donor from the family." Rosalie went to the kitchen sink to wash her hands. "I'm just worried about all of them. From what we were able to get out of the only person willing to talk about it, Arty's parents aren't suitable donors. One is in the process of undergoing dental treatment and the other has high blood pressure."

"Is Reba thinking about becoming a donor?" Alicia asked. "Wouldn't she be too old for that type of surgery?"

Rosalie shrugged. "Not if she's in good health, according to what I've heard and read recently." Rosalie felt as if lead weights had been tied to her feet. She was emotionally exhausted. "I also think Trina is having tests done," she whispered.

"Trina? Really?"

"She wouldn't tell me exactly. I asked her this afternoon, but all I got was a Trina answer."

"Be patient with her. I imagine she's got a lot on her mind."

"I know," Rosalie said.

When she left her parents' house she felt better, though still uneasy. She would make Trina talk to her.

Chapter Twenty Two

Rosalie was still upset as she got off the phone. Reba had told her she and Trina had gone in for tests that afternoon, and wouldn't know the results for a few days yet.

"I've learned a lot about kidneys recently," Reba said. "All you need is one, you know. It's like the Goddess gave us two so we could share one if we had to."

"So if you're a match," Rosalie said, "you'll give Arty a kidney?"

"Yes, I will. The transplant coordinator explained it all very well. That boy deserves the chance at a better life. It's not his fault he was raised by two homophobic bozos."

Rosalie became anxious just listening to Reba. She ended

the conversation and called Trina at work, asking her when she would be home.

"Not for a few more hours," Trina said. "The lounge is staying open the regular times, but I'm keeping the dining room open longer than usual. The hotel is absolutely packed. It's standing room only in the lobby even. If the fire department were to whiz in here they'd shut us down." Trina sighed; Rosalie could hear how tired she was. "Actually," Trina said, "if the Fire Chief were to arrive, I'd have no place to put him."

"So how long?" Rosalie asked. It was sounding like they wouldn't get to talk later after all. Rosalie could feel herself getting impatient. "Three hours? Four hours? Longer?"

"I don't know."

"Then will you at least wake me when you get home?"

"I can do that if you like."

"Please. I hate Fiesta, by the way. Have I mentioned that?"

"A few times," Trina said with a tired laugh. "I have to go."

Rosalie had a terrible time falling asleep. She was glad when she felt Trina slip into bed beside her and quietly ask if she was awake.

"What time is it?" Rosalie asked.

"A little after two."

Rosalie sat up in bed and turned on the lamp on the night stand. The light was a sudden harsh intrusion.

"What's the matter?" Trina asked.

"Let me see your arm."

"My what?"

Rosalie threw the covers off and reached over and turned Trina's arm so she could see it better. She found a small bruise from the needle where Trina had gotten a blood test earlier in the day.

"Why didn't you tell me you were getting tests done today?" Rosalie asked. She hadn't even realized she was crying.

"They just drew a little blood," Trina said, covering them up again with the sheet and a light blanket.

Rosalie snapped off the light and turned over with her back to Trina. When Trina didn't get settled in bed quite as quickly as Rosalie wanted her to, Rosalie said into the darkness, "I can't believe your arm isn't around me already."

Trina turned over and pressed the front of her body against Rosalie's back and slipped her arm around her.

"Is this better?" Trina whispered in her ear.

The closeness of Trina's lips as they brushed against Rosalie's ear sent a nice shiver through her body.

"Much better."

Trina kissed her gently on the neck just below her ear. "Please stop worrying."

"I have to worry," Rosalie said. "You don't tell me anything."

"I don't tell you anything because you worry so much."

Rosalie closed her eyes. Another wonderful shiver raced through her body as Trina slowly unbuttoned Rosalie's night shirt, slipped her hand inside and cupped her breast. Trina kissed Rosalie's neck, which sent a surge of heat swooshing through her veins.

"Tell me what you want right now," Trina whispered in that sultry, husky voice Rosalie loved to hear.

Rosalie turned over on her back and tilted her head so that Trina's lips could find more of her.

"Right now I want Arty to be well, and for you and Reba to keep your kidneys."

"That should happen if it's meant to be," Trina said.

Rosalie found Trina's mouth and kissed her hungrily. She

put her arms around her neck and pulled Trina on top of her. *I have to keep you safe,* Rosalie thought in a moment of desperation. *I want to . . . I need to . . . I have to.*

A few days later, Rosalie learned that Trina was the best possible match for Arty. Trina and Arty both had a blood type of AB, and a perfect antigen match as well. Rosalie had to hear all of this from Reba on the phone.

"Is she going to do it?" Rosalie asked. Just thinking about Trina losing a kidney made her teary, but actually talking about it made her feel nearly hysterical.

"They have to run more tests on her," Reba said, "but the transplant coordinator is in the process of setting them up now."

After work, she went home and waited for Trina. Rosalie had decided she wouldn't keep wondering what was going on. She had a vested interest in all of this and would demand to be part of it. Trina finally called her at six and said she was on her way home.

"What sounds good for dinner?" Trina asked.

"I'll make something quick for us," Rosalie said. She didn't want to go out or see anyone that evening. She and Trina would have a long night ahead of them.

"It smells good in here," Trina said when she came in the front door. She set her briefcase down at the end of the sofa and put her pager on top of it.

Rosalie avoided looking at her so Trina wouldn't be able to tell right away that she had been crying. There would be no way to hide it much longer, but Rosalie wanted to put it off as long as possible.

"By the time you get changed, dinner should be ready," Rosalie said. She went to the kitchen to get plates to set the table. Trina followed her and slipped up behind her, encircling Rosalie's waist with her arms.

"Please don't be angry," Trina whispered into her ear. "I can't do this without you."

Rosalie set the plates down on the counter and leaned back against her. She was crying again.

"I'm not angry, Trina. I'm frightened."

Trina's arms tightened around her.

"What if the surgery doesn't go well?" Rosalie asked. "What if some day you develop kidney problems and you only have one left?"

"Then I'll tell Arty that I need mine back," Trina said. She let go of her and left the kitchen. Rosalie followed her into the bedroom where Trina was changing clothes.

"Anything I know about this I've had to find out from Reba."

"I know," Trina said.

"Why can't you —" Rosalie's voice broke. She couldn't finish asking the question.

Trina slipped on a Regal Palace Hotel polo shirt and a pair of black jeans. She carefully hung up the skirt and jacket she had worn to work and stood in front of the closet just staring inside.

Rosalie snatched up a tissue from the night stand and wiped her eyes and blew her nose. When it became apparent Trina wasn't going to say anything else or even turn around, Rosalie attempted to find her voice again.

"Why can't you love me enough to want to share something like this with me?"

"Not love you enough?" Trina said. She turned around, tears welling up in her eyes. "How can you think that?"

"How? What other conclusion can I come to?" Rosalie asked. She felt so angry that she ached inside. "Reba, Juanito and Carmen knew more about your plans today than I did. And what about this transplant coordinator person? A total stranger knows more about your plans than I do! What am I to you, Trina? What have I ever been to you? This is just one more way for you to remind me how unimportant I am in your life! You're contemplating major surgery and I have to hear about the details from your family!"

Trina sat down on the edge of the bed with her back to Rosalie. She held her hand out for a moment and then covered her face with both of her hands and began to sob. Rosalie didn't know what to do at first; it broke her heart to see Trina reacting this way. Rosalie went around to the other side of the bed and knelt down in front of her, placing her hands on Trina's knees. Rosalie waited until the sobbing stopped, then she gently pulled Trina's hands away from her face.

"Talk to me, baby," Rosalie said.

Trina sniffed and rubbed her nose on the sleeve of her shirt. "You deal with children all day," Trina said haltingly, still trying to catch her breath. "Why can't you recognize child-like behavior in adults?"

"I can recognize it and still not like it," Rosalie said.

"Please sit next to me and hold me," Trina whispered.

Rosalie sat on the bed beside her.

"This won't do," Trina said. She crawled toward the center of the bed and took Rosalie into her arms. "First of all, I want to explain why I've been so weird about all of this. I never meant to ignore you or make you feel like you weren't important." Trina hugged her and began to cry again. They stayed that way for a long time until Trina settled down enough to continue.

"If Wesley, your only brother, needed a kidney and you were the best match for him, what would you do?" Trina asked.

"You mean after I discussed it thoroughly with you? My

lover?" Rosalie asked. They both chuckled and snuggled deeper into each others arms.

"Yes. After you discussed it with me, your lover."

"I would do whatever I could to save my brother's life," Rosalie said.

"That would be the noble thing to do," Trina said. "The natural thing to want to do. You love your brother. He loves you. I love *my* brother, but I can't say for sure that he cares about me." She took another deep breath. "But that's not what has been driving me with this decision." Trina hugged her fiercely. "I want Arty to have a lesbian's kidney. It's like that's the only part of this whole undertaking that makes me happy, and I'm not at all proud of any of those feelings. Do you understand what I'm saying?"

"You want to give your homophobic brother a lesbian's kidney. Trina, at this point in Arty's life he probably doesn't care who he gets a kidney from as long as the kidney he gets works."

"I'm sure you're right," Trina said, "but I'm afraid my motives have less to do with Arty's health than me needing to make a statement. That's the part that disturbs me the most right now."

"You've already admitted to me that you love your brother," Rosalie said. "Even though he's a jerk, he's still your brother."

"I know," Trina said. "I try not to even think about what my fate would be if our positions were reversed." She hugged Rosalie tightly again and kissed her on the forehead. "I'd be left trying to make a withdrawal at the kidney bank, I'm sure."

Rosalie swallowed the lump in her throat. She couldn't even convincingly tell Trina that she was wrong about that. Arty, more than likely, would not be having the same procedure done if their places were reversed.

"Anyway," Trina said. "The reason I haven't been able to talk to you about any of this is because I'm not proud of my reasons for wanting to do it."

"This is a brave thing you're considering, Trina. You also have to see I have a place in all of this with you."

"I was hoping you would say that," Trina whispered, "but I didn't know how to ask."

"You don't even have to ask. I want to be as involved as possible."

"Thank you," Trina said. She hugged her again. "How did I get so lucky to find you?"

Rosalie kissed her on the lips. "I think I must've been really, really bad in a former life."

Chapter Twenty Three

The next day after work, Rosalie and Trina met with the transplant coordinator, an RN named Eric Vega. Trina seemed more relaxed than Rosalie had seen her in a long time. Rosalie, on the other hand, was feeling even more anxious about the prospect of Trina having major surgery. She had read a number of articles on this type of operation, as well as a copy of *A Patient's Guide to Kidney Transplant Surgery*. The idea of Trina eventually having only one kidney frightened her, so it was Rosalie who went to the transplant coordinator's meeting prepared with the hard questions ... the questions she knew Trina hadn't given a second thought to yet ... the questions Rosalie wanted answers to before she could accept this decision Trina had made.

Eric Vega was a pleasant man in his mid-thirties. He was tall and fit, and sported a dark pencil-thin mustache. Having already heard Trina and Aunt Reba's description of him, Rosalie let their opinions influence her. She had heard good things about him already, and seemed to be very willing to accommodate their schedules. He was focused on making the early transplant procedures as uncomplicated as possible.

"Ms. Cofax," Eric said. "I understand you and Ms. LaRue are partners." He opened a folder on his desk. "Trina has you and Reba LaRue listed as the next of kin." He stopped and looked directly at Rosalie with a charming smile. "Don't they have the most delightful names? Trina and Reba LaRue. I just *love* that."

"We were both named after strippers," Trina said matter-of-factly.

Rosalie's eyes flew open at Eric's hearty laughter and she swatted Trina on the arm. "You were not! You're always telling people that."

Still chuckling, Eric informed them he had several documents for Trina to fill out. "Then I'll go over some of the tests I'll be scheduling you for during the next few days." He handed them both a list of medical tests Trina would be taking. "Now that we know you're a match for Arty, it's imperative we get a clear picture of your overall health status. If we can identify any potential problems right away, it will increase the likelihood of a successful transplant."

"So even though Trina and Arty are a match," Rosalie said, "the transplant may not work?" Once again, she could hear the anxiety in her voice and realized she needed to calm down.

"Yes, there's a chance Arty's body might reject Trina's

kidney or any kidney, for that matter," Eric said. "We'll give him drugs to lessen those chances, but it could still happen."

"It's okay," Trina said quietly, squeezing Rosalie's hand.

"I'm sorry," Rosalie said. She knew she had to settle down. She had too many questions to ask to get this upset over the first one.

"A kidney from a relative usually means there is less chance of rejection and Arty might not have to take as much medication." Eric pointed toward the sheet of paper he had given them. "This is your pre-transplant evaluation check list. We need to make sure that you're free from disease, infection, or injury that affects your kidneys." To Trina he said, "We've already completed the blood typing and the crossmatch testing on you. The remaining tests listed can be done next week at your convenience."

Rosalie scanned the list of things Trina would have to have done, which included a chest x-ray, an ultrasound with doppler exam, a pulmonary function test, an upper and lower GI series, a mammogram, a pap smear, an electrocardiogram, echocardiogram, a dental examination and viral testing. Thinking about all these preliminaries was making Rosalie feel better for some reason. She liked the idea of Trina getting all the tests done, even though some would not be pleasant. It would be nice to know Trina was in good physical condition, just for her own personal peace of mind.

"Will my insurance pay for all of this?" Trina asked.

"Your brother's insurance will pay for everything. That includes your tests, the surgery and any follow-up that you'll need."

"When will we get the results back?" Rosalie asked.

"By the end of next week," Eric said. "Arty is having most of the same tests done, so once we get all the results in, I'd like to meet with you and your brother together so we can pinpoint a date for the surgery."

"Is that necessary?" Trina asked, letting go of Rosalie's hand. "Can't we just pick a date? All you have to do is tell me where to be and what time to be there. We don't need a meeting."

"It's customary I get both of you together and go over the surgery and answer any questions either of you might have."

Rosalie decided to let Trina handle this part of the interview. The working dynamics of the LaRue family were complicated at best.

"I'd prefer just to have a date for the surgery," Trina said. "I've made arrangements to be off from work for the recovery period. I'm flexible with all of that. There's no need for a meeting."

"Is there a problem here that I don't know about?" Eric asked.

Trina didn't answer. Rosalie wasn't sure it was her place to get into it.

"No meeting," Trina said finally.

"I don't understand."

"My brother and I are not close. A meeting wouldn't be a good idea."

"Then let me suggest that we also engage in a few sessions with a counselor." He scribbled something down on a pad of paper. "That can be arranged easily and should be something that can help keep Arty's spirits high."

"You don't understand," Trina said. "I'm not having a meeting and I'm not going into therapy with my brother."

Eric set his pen down. "This isn't about you, Ms. LaRue. This is about your brother, who could die from renal failure. We need to do what's best for him."

"The way I see it," Trina said simply, "is that this is about Arty's bad kidneys and about one of my *good* kidneys. You and Arty can work on his mental state. I'll do the tests and I'll have the surgery, but I'm not wasting my time or my energy on therapy or a meeting."

Rosalie reached for Trina's hand again and laced their fingers together. She watched as Eric scribbled something else on the tablet.

"May I ask you why you're agreeing to give your brother such a wonderful gift?" Eric asked. "You're willing to give him a kidney, but you won't even meet with him?"

"Do you people want my kidney or not?" Trina asked. "If not, then just say so. I can take my kidneys and my lover and go home."

"I'm here to do what's best for Arty. His needs are where our focus has to be."

"Have you checked with Arty about whether or not he wants to meet with us?" Rosalie asked. "You might have to change the way you do a few things. The LaRue's are not your average family."

"I'm beginning to see that," Eric said with a frown.

"No meeting," Trina said.

"This is against policy and my recommendation."

"A meeting with me will only upset Arty," Trina said. "I know you can arrange the surgery without a meeting with us."

Eric looked at Trina for a long time before finally saying, "Then let me see what I can do about getting all the information together I want you and your brother to be familiar with."

To Rosalie's surprise, Trina brought their entwined hands up to her lips and kissed the back of Rosalie's fingers.

As the days passed, Rosalie was relieved Trina chose to be more open with her about what was going on. Rosalie drove her to all of her appointments. They talked about things in a way Rosalie had never thought possible before. They invited Aunt Reba, Juanito and Carmen over for dinner one night and officially told them about Trina's decision to give Arty one of her kidneys. When Aunt Reba began to cry, Rosalie started to cry too.

"After everything that little turd's done to you," Reba said with a sniff as she gave her niece a fierce hug.

"All of that sort of evened itself out when I stole his girlfriend," Trina reminded her.

Juanito gave them a stern look and asked if they were starting up with that turd talk again, which made Reba laugh. Over a fine meal of poached salmon, cucumber salad and Rosalie's homemade macaroni and cheese, the women worked out the details of Trina's recovery. The first few days she would be out of the hospital, it was decided Aunt Reba would stay with them. Trina would be off work for nearly six weeks, but she would only need help the first week she was home. With the school year coming to an end soon, Rosalie and Trina would be able to spend more time together during her recovery period.

The next evening over another dinner at Rosalie and Trina's house, they also told the Cofaxes about the transplant. Rosalie was still amazed at how calm Trina was when she talked about the surgery . . . as if giving away a kidney was something she did every day! Rosalie was still torn between wanting Arty to be well and for Trina to keep all of her organs. *Who's to say Trina won't some day need that extra kidney for herself,* she thought.

"I think it's a very courageous thing you're doing, Trina," Peter Cofax said.

"Hmm. I don't think of it that way at all," Trina said. "I certainly don't feel courageous. The reactions I've been getting from people have really surprised me, though. My boss has been supportive and that's really what will make the whole thing possible. I need the time off from work and I didn't get any hassle about taking it."

"She's become a Regal Palace celebrity," Rosalie said. She also saw this as an unselfish, courageous act. Rosalie liked knowing her father thought of it that way, too. "They're doing an article on her to help promote the Regal Palace's support of their Family Leave policy."

"I'm like the kidney donor poster child for the corporation," Trina said. "My boss even wants to throw a party for me. He told me about it today. He's calling it the 'Saying Good-bye to Trina's Kidney' party."

Rosalie could see the amusement in Trina's eyes. She wondered if Trina was truly aware of the seriousness of what she was about to do. Rosalie made a mental note to try and get her to talk more about her feelings. The longer she thought about Eric Vega's suggestion in reference to therapy before the surgery, the better it was starting to sound to her. Rosalie wanted Trina to be prepared to accept the fact that neither Arty nor the LaRues would show any type of gratitude for what she was going to do. Rosalie wanted to be sure Trina was mentally ready to deal with further rejection from her family.

Trina laughed. "You should have heard them talking about the party menu. Kidney beans, key lime kidney pie, sundaes with a nice pineapple sauce topping, giving the ice cream that fresh urine look. They were quite creative. I vetoed the pineapple sauce topping thing, though. It was one of those brainstorming gross afterthoughts."

"I think the party is a great idea," Alicia Cofax said, "and having the support of your boss has to make all of this easier. In these types of situations, I can see how the Family Leave Act will make a difference in a lot of people's lives."

Rosalie watched her mother make her way across the living room and give Trina a warm hug. Rosalie felt that familiar lump return to her throat. She wished that just once Trina's own mother could show her that kind of love.

Chapter Twenty Four

The surgery was scheduled for the following week. All of the tests had been completed and the results were in. Wanting to spend some quality time together, Rosalie and Trina preferred staying at home, so they hosted dinners at their house when their friends or family wanted to see them. Along with all the medical tests that Trina was going through, they had also seen a lawyer and had gotten their wills taken care of. Included was the Medical Directive to the Physician paperwork, in case there were unexpected complications during or after Trina's surgery.

"I'm sorry," Rosalie said during one of their preliminary discussions about this. "I couldn't tell them to pull the plug on you if you stopped responding to treatment. I want those people working on you until their arms fall off."

"I'm in excellent physical shape," Trina said. "One kidney will already be gone. If something happens and I'm no longer 'me', then I want to be an organ donor."

"Sorry," Rosalie said again, tearing up one more time. *Why are we still having these conversations?* she wondered. "I can't do it. Have Reba be the one to sign your life away. *Your* wishes are not *my* wishes."

So when they had Aunt Reba, Carmen and Juanito over for dinner a few nights later, Rosalie was happy to see Reba was even more appalled at the prospect of being the one to decide Trina's fate in the event there were complications during or after the surgery.

"You'd better not stick *my* name on that form if you want to give up on yourself that way," Reba said. "I've read about things like this, Trina. They don't try as hard to save you if they know you're an organ donor."

"So you won't agree to look out for my interests either?" Trina asked.

"I'm with Rosalie on this one," Aunt Reba said. "If I get a vote, then they'll keep resuscitating and there won't be any more organ loans from you."

Rosalie chuckled along with everyone else. Having the uncontrollable urge to touch her again, Rosalie reached for Trina's hand.

"Then there's that lack of brain activity thing they do," Aunt Reba said. "They would need to verify that there had been any brain activity to begin with, wouldn't you think?"

"So what exactly is it that you want?" Juanito asked Trina. He stood near the fireplace holding a glass of grape Kool-Aid. "If they get in there and screw something up —"

"Oy," Rosalie said, rolling her eyes. There she was again in the middle of one of those doom and gloom conversations.

"As I was saying," Juanito continued. "What is it that you

want, Trina?" To the others in the room he said, "These would be her last wishes. Why wouldn't any of you want that for her?"

"I want her alive," Rosalie said. She knew her voice was giving away her emotions. "I want her alive with *all* of her body parts intact."

"That's what *you* want," Juanito said. "This isn't about what you want."

"Thank you!" Trina said. "So I guess now I know who gets to be named on my Medical Directive of the Physician paperwork."

"Oh, no!" Juanito said emphatically, waving his arms in the air. "You're not leaving me here to face these two alone," he said, pointing to Rosalie and Reba.

"Well, fuck," Trina said.

Rosalie was in bed, waiting for Trina to finish a phone call. It was four days until the surgery. All Rosalie could think about was being with her and holding her. Feeling as though she had no more tears left, Rosalie had resigned herself to the fact this was going to happen, and Trina needed for her to be stronger.

She watched Trina hang up the phone, still smiling from her conversation with her Aunt Reba.

"What are they up to tonight?" Rosalie asked.

"She's on a rampage about my Aunt Missy," Trina said. "It seems as though no one is talking about the donor." She was clearly amused by this. Rosalie continued to be puzzled by Trina's reaction to all of it. "That's what my new name is now, you know." She sat down on the edge of the bed and took off her shoes. "I'm no longer 'That Girl' or 'That Queer Girl.' I'm now 'The Donor.' "

Rosalie reached over and touched Trina's back. "How can you be so calm about all of this? Why aren't you angry with them?" She was disappointed that neither Arty nor any of the LaRues had been in touch with Trina.

"I traded all my anger in a long time ago," Trina said. She stood up and took off her jeans and draped them over a chair. On her way back to bed she unbuttoned her shirt and took it off also. "If Aunt Reba hadn't put me in therapy when I first went to live with them, I'm not sure I would be here now. I've dealt with my family's rejection most of my life. I've accepted it and I've moved on. I have a relapse for a few minutes during December each year, but it's like I need that to remind myself about where I've been and where I'd rather be."

As she lay down, Rosalie let her eyes slowly roam over Trina's body. Her firm breasts had such a nice round shape to them even when she was laying on her back. Just on the edge of being aroused, her nipples were dark and slightly puckered. Rosalie took in the sight of her pale skin and flat stomach, letting her eyes slowly trace every inch of her as she tried to burn the image of Trina's body into her mind. There were no blemishes, staples, stitches or scars. Rosalie knew after the surgery she would do this again.

"Are you just going to look?" Trina whispered. "You're killing me here. Kiss me or something."

"I plan to do that and much more, baby." Rosalie leaned over and touched the tip of her tongue to Trina's left nipple. "Much, much more."

Rosalie was happy to see such a large number of people attending the "Saying Good-bye to Trina's Kidney" party at the Regal Palace. There were even several people from the hotel in Dallas where Trina used to work, as well as all of Rosalie's friends from the Teacher's Support Group. Roscoe Hobart and his wife were also there, along with the Regional Director for the Regal Palace Hotel chain. There were constant camera flashes and camcorders everywhere, an open bar and a huge kidney-shaped cake in the center of a conference table.

The details of the evening were being tended to by Dee Cockran, which left Trina to just concentrate on relaxing and having a good time. At Trina's insistence, Rosalie stayed by her side where they held hands all evening. Rosalie's parents were there also, talking to several of the teachers from the support group.

Earlier, Juanito had started the evening off by turning Trina around and kissing both sides of her lower back where he decided her kidneys were. After that, every time someone new arrived at the party, they had to do the same thing. As the night wore on, Rosalie could plainly see various shades of lipstick imprinted on Trina's apricot-colored blouse. Some well-wishers even went back more than once to bless Trina's kidneys with their lips.

"I don't know how to thank you for all of this, Roscoe," Trina said. She was still holding Rosalie's hand as they stood there side by side. Rosalie instinctively leaned into her so she could be closer to her.

"It's my pleasure, Trina," Roscoe said. "This is such a wonderful thing you're doing for your brother. You're also giving us some excellent publicity with the corporate office, not to mention management and employee relations. They all love this story." He gave Trina a pat on the shoulder. "Take as much time as you need to recover from the surgery. We have things under control here."

"There you two are," Wesley said from behind Rosalie. She gave her brother a hug and pointed to the back of Trina's blouse.

"You have to kiss both kidneys," Rosalie said. "We're not sure which one is leaving."

Wesley grinned and kissed the two places on Trina's back where Rosalie pointed.

"Officer Cofax," Trina said. Rosalie smiled as Trina introduced him to the Hobarts as her brother-in-law. "It's good to have you here!"

"I've seen the cake already," Wesley said. "Do you think anyone will want to eat it?"

"Let's go cut it and see," Trina said. "They've gotten more than enough cake pictures already."

Trina and Roscoe went over to the table where the cake was. Rosalie watched her make her way through the crowd while several people continued to bless her kidneys with kisses.

"How are you holding up?" Wesley asked Rosalie.

She shrugged. "I'm nervous and worried, but other than that I'm okay."

"I'm taking off the day of the surgery," he said. "I want to be there with you. Mom and Dad will be there, too."

On impulse, she hugged him again. All Rosalie seemed to do lately was cry. "Thank you."

There was a swell of laughter and Rosalie looked over to see Trina and Roscoe having a cake-cutting ceremony in the middle of the room. Rosalie brushed away her tears and followed her brother to get a piece of cake. Once she was close enough to see her better, Rosalie noticed that the back of Trina's blouse was now totally covered with various shades of lipstick and lip imprints.

All that remained were a few crumbs left from the cake, some broken tortilla chips in the various bowls, and a cold plate of nachos. Trina had sent the bartender home about thirty minutes earlier, but several people still weren't ready to call it a night yet. Rosalie's parents, Aunt Reba and Carmen had just left, but Juanito, Naomi and her lover Marcel were still there. Everyone had gravitated to the center of the room and were sitting around the huge conference table, all deep in conversation with the Hobarts. Rosalie was tired, but the party had been a good idea. It was obvious to her now even though the transplant was a serious operation, there was also a place for some fun and laughter. That was how Trina seemed to want to approach this, and Rosalie was learning to respect that.

As she got closer to the table to join them, Rosalie heard Nelda Hobart ask Trina what her most memorable hotel experience had been.

"We all have them," Nelda said. "One morning we had a naked guest who locked himself out of his room by accident. When someone finally went up to let him in again, he had two copies of *USA Today* covering himself up. One in front and one in back."

Rosalie sat down next to Trina and liked the way Trina automatically put her arm along the back of Rosalie's chair and then let her fingers mingle in her hair.

"When I first started out in this business I caught two of my friends skinny dipping in the hotel pool one night," Roscoe said. "We all worked in food service together. I swam in that pool too sometimes! That kind of ticked me off, so I took their clothes when they weren't looking. I got their car keys and everything."

"What happened to them?" Naomi asked.

"They were stuck there until a guest came out to go for a swim."

"I got robbed once," Trina said. Her fingers slowly moved deeper into Rosalie's hair and touched the back of her neck in a light caress.

"I bet that was scary," Nelda said.

Juanito started to laugh, which then made Trina laugh.

"Oh, yes," Trina said. "It was very scary. I worked at a Holiday Inn when I first started. There was a Ramada Inn just down the road from us and a friend of mine worked there. It was about two in the morning and my boss had some paperwork to do in the back. She would let me do my school work if we weren't busy. I was still going to college then. It was dead quiet that night and I was just about finished with an economics take-home test." Trina laughed again. "Anyway, I gave my friend at the Ramada a call. We were taking the same class together and sometimes we'd do our homework over the phone. All of a sudden this huge guy comes in. He must've been about six-eight and all I could think of when I saw him was that Grizzly Adams was checking in. Then he pulled out a pistol that I swear had to have been about three feet long. 'Gimme da money,' he says. I dropped the phone and started to shake." Trina smiled. "I was shaking so hard I couldn't pull the money out of the register, but I finally got it all out and he told me to put it in a brown paper sack he had with him. So I stuffed all the money in the bag. 'You want the change too?' I asked him." Trina tossed her head back and laughed again. " '*All* da money,' he said. So I finally got all the change scooped up, too."

Rosalie put her hand on Trina's knee under the table. She loved hearing her tell this story. Each time Trina told it she added something new.

"So I'm still shaking and I can hear my friend Consuelo on the phone that's dangling there and she's saying, 'Does he have a gun? Trina! Does he have a gun?' Then the guy says to me, 'Now gimme your purse. I know you keep it under the counter there.' So I look under the counter and I see my purse and I see my boss's purse. Guess which one I gave him?"

"Your boss's purse!" Nelda Hobart said, just before everyone at the table howled with laughter.

By the time they were all ready to call it a night, Rosalie was exhausted. She fell asleep on Trina's shoulder as Trina drove them home.

Chapter Twenty Five

The day before the surgery Rosalie took Trina to the hospital for pre-admission, where they got her checked in and settled. Earlier that day, Rosalie had called Eric Vega to make sure he understood that Trina didn't want to be in a room close to Arty's.

"Put them at opposite ends of the hospital if you can," Rosalie had told him.

He still seemed to be having problems understanding the dynamics of the LaRue family, even though the situation had been thoroughly explained to him. Rosalie made it a point to remind him she didn't care if he agreed with why things were a certain way. She just wanted to make sure Trina didn't have to deal with that part of her family right now.

Rosalie stayed with her that evening until the staff told her she had to leave. Aunt Reba and Juanito had been there earlier and promised to be back in the morning. Rosalie didn't want to leave Trina alone. If she had been able to get away with crawling in that bed with her and just curling herself around Trina's body, she would have done so and felt better, but the nursing staff was getting annoyed.

"Will you be able to sleep?" Rosalie asked. She pulled up the sheet and a thin blanket and tucked Trina in snugly.

"I'll be fine," Trina said. "Please stop worrying." She reached up and touched Rosalie's cheek. "I'm sorry I'm putting you through this."

"Don't be sorry," Rosalie whispered. She had promised herself she wouldn't let Trina see her cry again. It only made her feel bad. But unfortunately, she couldn't stop a tear from scampering down her cheek now. "If you only knew how proud I am of you." Touching the side of Trina's head, Rosalie moved a stray lock of auburn hair away from Trina's forehead. "If you only knew how much I love you."

Rosalie watched Trina's eyes fill with tears. "I know," Trina whispered. "I see it every day."

Eric Vega came into the room with a clipboard under his arm. "How are we doing this evening?"

"We're doing fine," Trina said.

"I was just going," Rosalie said. *Having him here will make it easier to leave her now,* she thought. "Good night, baby," Rosalie said. Not giving a second thought as to who was in the room with them, she leaned over and kissed her. "I'll be back in the morning." On Rosalie's way out of the room she told Eric to make sure Trina had everything she needed. "Please," she added. "And I mean everything."

Rosalie hadn't gotten much sleep. She had barely crawled into bed when Trina called her from her hospital room. They

217

had talked until a nurse came in to shave Trina's pubic area. One of the last things Rosalie heard her say before hanging up was, "Can you give it a nice heart shape down there? I want to surprise my girlfriend." An hour later, when Trina called her back, she was impressed at how professional the nurse had been. "Neither one of us was embarrassed," Trina said. "I'm still not sure how she pulled that off."

They talked until they were both sleepy. Rosalie couldn't help but notice how big the bed was without Trina there with her. She was up before the alarm went off, and on her way to the hospital before the morning rush-hour traffic began. Getting there early was like an obsession. Rosalie wasn't going to be intimidated by scowling nurses.

"Good morning, baby," Rosalie said as she kissed Trina on the lips. "Are you doing okay?"

"I have a bald snatch," Trina said.

"Can I see it?"

Trina pulled the covers up around her chin. "Now I'm embarrassed."

Rosalie laughed. "No need for that. It'll be one of the first things we'll explore together when I get you home, okay?"

It didn't take long for things to start happening. They saw Eric Vega only briefly; Rosalie realized he was spending most of his time in Arty's room. At first she couldn't help being miffed by all the attention Arty was getting, but remembered Arty's life was hanging in the balance. He was the one who was ill. She reminded herself again that Arty's needs had to be taken care of first.

Trina was upbeat and didn't seem at all concerned with what was about to happen. Rosalie thought Trina looked beautiful with her reddish-tinted hair being such a nice contrast against the white pillow on the bed. Rosalie followed behind the bed the two orderlies were guiding down the hallway.

Once they got Trina to another area where there were other patients waiting for surgery, Rosalie saw something different in Trina's eyes. Even though she was getting something new in the IV now, Rosalie understood Trina should be more relaxed than she seemed to be. It didn't take long for her to become alarmed when Trina grabbed her by the hand and squeezed hard.

"I can hear them," Trina said.

"Who, baby?"

"My father. I can hear him talking."

There had to be twenty or so beds in the huge room, with curtains pulled around most of them. Arty would be there somewhere as well, his own entourage there with him.

"I'll be right back," Rosalie said. She gave Trina's hand another squeeze and went to look for Eric. If Arty was there, then Eric couldn't be far away.

Rosalie asked the first person she saw in scrubs if he could page Eric or lead her to him. Before having to do either of those things, Rosalie saw him and waved him over.

"Are the LaRues here?" she asked. "Trina can hear them and it's upsetting her."

"Of course they're here. I have Arty at the opposite end of the room per your request. I'm doing my part, Ms. Cofax."

"Then can you tell them to be quiet?"

"They *are* quiet. Maybe Trina is just imagining she hears them."

Rosalie wasn't going to get into that with him. *If Trina says she heard her father, then she heard her father.*

"All I know is that she's getting agitated and I don't want her upset now. I'm sure you don't either."

"Let me go over and talk to her," Eric said.

Rosalie caught him by the arm. "I'll take care of Trina. All you need to do is keep the LaRues quiet."

She left him standing there hugging his clipboard. Rosalie went back to Trina's bed and vowed not to cry in front of her again. She was too angry to cry now anyway.

* * * * *

After they wheeled Trina away, Rosalie went to the waiting room and was happy to see Juanito and Aunt Reba there already. Juanito handed her a Styrofoam cup of coffee.

"Carmen is parking the car," he said. "We brought tacos if you get hungry."

She hugged them both and sat down in the chair between them. Before Rosalie could tell them about what had happened so far that morning, her parents and her brother arrived.

"What have we missed so far?" Peter Cofax asked.

Rosalie was so glad to have them there she calmed down immediately. As she gave her report about what had happened since she had arrived, Juanito passed around the bag full of breakfast tacos. There was nothing else to do but wait. However, an hour or so later when the door to the waiting area opened and the LaRues came in, Rosalie's anger returned almost immediately. The LaRues seemed just as shocked to see Trina's support group there.

As if an imaginary line had been drawn down the middle of the room, the LaRues stayed as far away as possible. Then two at a time, the rest of the LaRue family began to arrive. Rosalie recognized Trina's aunts and uncles from a few family gatherings she attended with Arty when they had been dating. Rosalie then saw the blonde Trina had described to her on Christmas Day. That had to be Pam, Arty's new girlfriend. Rosalie watched nervously as both of her parents got up and went over to talk to the LaRues.

"Don't they know they're consorting with the enemy?" Rosalie heard Juanito whisper with a chuckle.

"Think of it as a fact-finding mission," Aunt Reba whispered back.

The next time Rosalie saw Eric Vega he was there speaking for the transplant surgeon.

"Trina's fine," Eric said. "She's in ICU now. She'll be there until the anesthesia wears off. Once she comes out of it, there should be some pain and discomfort, but we'll have her on something to take care of that."

"When can I see her?" Rosalie asked with a sniff. She was trembling, but relieved.

"I'll let you know when they take her back to her room," Eric said, "or you can go there and wait for her if you like."

Eric left and went directly over to the LaRues. That irritated Rosalie for some reason; she wanted out of there quickly.

"I'm going back to her room to wait," Rosalie said. Suddenly plagued with anxiety, she just wanted to see Trina again no matter what shape she was in.

Rosalie sent everyone home once they all saw for themselves Trina was all right. Trina was heavily sedated and wasn't aware of how many people were concerned about her. Rosalie convinced them to leave and visit the next day. Everyone agreed, except for Aunt Reba.

"You look so tired," Rosalie said as she hugged Reba. "Are you sure you want to stay?"

"We can both watch her sleep," Reba said. "I would be miserable at home."

So, they stayed in Trina's room and waited. Later that afternoon, Eric come in and told them Arty's new kidney was already functioning and early indications were that the transplant was a success. For Rosalie, it was a relief to know Trina wasn't going through all this for nothing. She was also glad Arty would be feeling better soon.

Eventually Trina woke up and drifted in and out of a drug-induced sleep.

"How do you feel, baby?" Rosalie asked her at one point.

"It hurts," Trina whispered.

Rosalie pushed the button on the IV and released more of

the pain killer. Trina looked pale. Even in her sleep she was grimacing. Rosalie felt someone beside her, and then Reba took Rosalie's hand as they both stood there looking at Trina asleep in the bed.

"Why do you think she wanted to do this?" Reba asked. She slipped a wadded up tissue out of her pocket and dabbed her nose. "Besides wanting to give that boy a lesbian's kidney."

Rosalie let go of Reba's hand and put her arm around her waist.

"She wants the approval and love of her family," Rosalie said. "That's all she's ever wanted."

"The chances of that happening are very slim," Reba said. "Leopards can't change their spots."

Rosalie loved the way Trina's eyes lit up each time more flowers were delivered. Her room was full of them. She had visitors in and out all day long. Trina's boss had been by, as well as several of her employees and coworkers.

"How do you feel?" Juanito asked, two days after the surgery.

"Like a shark bit me," Trina said. She motioned for Juanito to come closer and then whispered something to him. Rosalie watched as he threw his head back and laughed.

"No, no," he said. "Not me! Get someone else to do it. Or send her an email."

"What does she want you to do?" Rosalie asked him a few minutes later.

Juanito leaned over and whispered, "She wants me to go tell Arty's girlfriend he'll be a better lover now that he has a lesbian's kidney."

Rosalie glanced over at the bed, but Trina was busy talking to her Aunt Reba.

"She's frisky already," Juanito said. "She'll be fine."

Eric came in. Rosalie smiled when she saw Juanito checking him out.

"I didn't recognize you without your clipboard," Trina said to him.

"How are you feeling?" Eric asked.

"Like someone removed one of my kidneys," Trina said. "They're giving me excellent drugs, though."

"I have someone here who would like to see you." Eric went back to the door and escorted Mercedes LaRue, Trina's mother, into the room.

Rosalie's heart began to race and the room was now eerily quiet. No one moved except Mrs. LaRue who came around the end of Trina's bed and stood beside it. Mercedes was more relaxed than she had been the day of the surgery.

"I want to personally thank you for saving your brother's life," she said. Her voice had a slight tremor to it, much like Trina's did when she was upset. "It was a courageous and totally unselfish thing you did. How are you feeling, dear?"

"Fine," Trina said in a low, husky voice.

"Your father wants to see you when he gets off work later, if that would be all right."

"Sure," Trina said. "I'll be here."

"This has been a terrible ordeal," Mercedes said to everyone in the room. Then to Trina she said, "Your father and I want to do better. He's been to see Father Eddie and now has a better understanding about the things he's done. I'm sorry I wasn't a stronger person and more protective of you, but to go against your father . . . well . . . I made a terrible mistake letting him have his way like that back then. I'll do better. We'll do better."

Rosalie thought the woman was going to cry, but she didn't. However, her voice was still brimming with emotion. It was as though everyone in the room was in shock. Eric came over and stood at the end of Trina's bed.

"We'll be back later when Mr. LaRue gets here," Eric said. He took Mercedes gently by the arm and escorted her out.

To Rosalie, it felt like the room itself let go with a giant sigh of relief. Juanito and Aunt Reba looked at each other as if not knowing what to say. Rosalie went directly to Trina and leaned over the bed railing and hugged her. Trina put her arms around Rosalie's neck and cried softly.

Chapter Twenty Six

The next morning, Rosalie found Arty in Trina's room sitting in a chair next to her bed. He nodded and smiled when he saw her. Rosalie looked at Trina, who was sitting up in bed with a calm, relaxed expression on her face. When the nursing staff had finally insisted Rosalie leave the night before, she had called Trina on her cell phone before she was even out of the hospital. Rosalie had been upset about having to leave her alone. Trina's father hadn't shown up before visiting hours were over. Trina had been on an emotional roller coaster after seeing her mother earlier in the evening, and Rosalie wanted to be with her and help her get through it. They had stayed on the phone together until Trina finally fell asleep.

"I was just telling Trina that I can pee again," Arty said. He and Trina both laughed.

"I'm glad to hear that," Rosalie said, chuckling along with them. "It's very good to see you here, Arty." She moved to the side of Trina's bed and reached for her hand. If there was going to be any type of relationship between the three of them, Rosalie wanted it understood right away that she was Trina's lover — not her friend, not her roommate, not her housemate, but her lover. "So you're feeling better?"

"I feel great," Arty said. "It hurts where they cut me open, but I can pee on my own. That's the most important thing."

Rosalie recognized that boyish smile he had. She was beginning to see the Arty she had once thought she was in love with.

"I was telling Trina that Dad had to work late yesterday," he said. "He's been really busy since I've been too sick to help him at the shop."

"I see."

Arty's blue pajamas and matching robe were both starched and looked new. Rosalie imagined his mother had been tending to his hospital wardrobe.

"I don't know how to thank you for what you've done for me, Trina," Arty said.

"You don't have to thank me," Trina said quietly.

"I think just having you here is a good start, Arty," Rosalie said.

He hung his head and nodded. Arty then said to Trina, "You need to get up and walk around some. It gets easier the more you do it. Getting up sucks, but once I'm up I do okay getting around." He used both arms on the chair and got himself out of it. "See?" Arty said, looking pale for a few moments. "That sucked big time, but it's okay now." To Rosalie he said, "Make her walk around this place some."

"I will," Rosalie said.

"It's your turn to come and visit me now," he said. "I need to get back. I don't want to miss breakfast."

"I have a question for you, Arty," Trina said.

He had shuffled to the end of her bed and stopped there. "What is it?"

"I was just wondering if you still pee standing up now that you have a lesbian's kidney."

"Damn, Trina," he said.

To Rosalie's surprise Arty laughed.

"There you go starting with me already," he said. "Come and see me after breakfast. Room 302b." Then to Rosalie, he said, "Both of you come and see me."

Rosalie sent Juanito and Aunt Reba ahead with all the plants and flowers. Trina was well enough to go home, but wasn't happy with the clothes Rosalie had brought for her to wear home from the hospital.

"I say we roll you out of here in your nightgown and robe," Rosalie said. "You can't wear sweats yet unless I get them five sizes too big and then keep them up with suspenders. Nothing should be touching the incision."

"I know. I know," Trina grumbled, "but I'm tired of looking all frumpy."

Rosalie smiled and wanted to hug her. "You look beautiful, silly. Who said you looked frumpy?"

"I did," Trina said. She tossed her brush into her suitcase, and then stopped what she was doing.

Rosalie looked up and saw Arthur LaRue, Trina's father, there in his work clothes.

"Rosalie," he said with a nod. "Can I have a word with my daughter?"

"She can stay," Trina said. She put her house shoes in the suitcase and slipped on her loafers. "Arty said you were working."

"I couldn't get here any sooner," he said, "but I wanted to see you before you went home."

"Then you just caught me."

He came around the end of the bed and put his arms around her. Trina hugged him and then started to cry.

"You saved your brother's life," he said. "All on your own."

Rosalie also began to cry as she stood there watching them. A hospital volunteer came in with a wheelchair. Trina released her grip on him and let him help her get in the wheelchair.

"Can I take her out?" he asked the frail, elderly volunteer.

"Hospital policy says I have to do it," the woman said sweetly.

"You can carry this while I go get the car," Rosalie said as she zipped up the suitcase and handed it over to him. She glanced at Trina in the wheelchair to see if she was all right, but Trina wasn't looking at her. Rosalie knelt down beside her and asked if she was okay.

"Yes," Trina whispered. "Just take me home."

Rosalie went to get the car. By the time she drove back to the main entrance, Trina was there in the wheelchair, her eyes looking straight ahead. The volunteer and Arthur LaRue were standing behind Trina chatting away. Rosalie leaned over from the driver's side and opened the passenger's door. Arthur helped his daughter get in the car and fasten her seat belt.

"You take care of her," he said to Rosalie.

"I plan to."

He shut the car door and Rosalie drove away. Trina seemed to be in shock; she was too still and too quiet.

"Are you okay, baby?" Rosalie whispered.

"Get a good look at him in the rearview mirror. We'll probably never see any of them again."

"Did he really?" Aunt Reba asked later that evening. She fluffed up Trina's pillow, and got her settled in on the sofa in

Rosalie and Trina's living room. "Well, I never thought I'd see the day when those two turds would come around."

Rosalie, Trina and Reba all three looked over at Juanito, who was across the room separating the live flowers from the dead ones in the various arrangements.

"Yes, I heard more turd talk coming from you over there," he said.

"Well, would *you* have believed it?" Reba asked him.

"Not really," Juanito said, "but strange things happen to people sometimes. Maybe they had a religious experience or something. Almost losing a child can make a lot of things suddenly seem trivial."

Rosalie still wasn't comfortable with how quiet Trina was. The doctor had her on something for the pain, but she hadn't taken anything yet. When Trina waved her over to the sofa, Rosalie was there beside her right away.

"Can you get Eric Vega on the phone for me?"

"Sure," Rosalie said. "Are you okay? Are you hurting anywhere?" He was the point of contact for any post-operative complications Trina might have.

"I'm fine," Trina said. "I just want to talk to him."

Rosalie called Eric's cell phone number and handed Trina the phone. Rosalie stayed by her side while she talked to him.

"Eric, it's Trina LaRue. What did you do to my parents and my brother? All three of them are suddenly being nice to me."

Rosalie watched Trina lean back against her fluffed pillow and smile as she listened on the phone.

"You put them in therapy," Trina said. "They agreed to go on their own?" She glanced over at Rosalie. For the first time in days, Rosalie saw the old Trina return. "I see. Well, you did an excellent job, Eric. I appreciate everything you've done." She turned the phone off and gave it back to Rosalie.

"So what did he say?" Rosalie asked.

"Apparently they didn't believe I was the donor until they saw all of you in the waiting room during Arty's surgery."

"Who did they think it was?" Reba asked. "Eric told them. Missy knew. That woman surely can't keep a secret!"

"I'm just telling you what Eric said. He doesn't know if they were in denial or if they just spaced out together," Trina said, "but something happened to them when they saw you guys in the waiting room and finally realized they had two kids in surgery at the same time."

"They aren't just turds," Reba said. "They're stupid turds."

There was a knock on the door and Rosalie went to answer it. She looked out the window and saw Mercedes and Arthur LaRue standing on the porch. She opened the door and invited them in. Rosalie was happy that Trina's earlier prediction about never seeing them again wouldn't be coming true.

"Come in!" Rosalie said. "How nice to see you both again. Trina's there on the sofa."

They both came in and were visibly nervous. Rosalie thought it best to make this as painless as possible for everyone. Juanito had already disappeared into the kitchen. That left Rosalie as the buffer — the one willing to do whatever it would take to make this work and less uncomfortable.

"How are you feeling, dear?" her mother asked Trina.

"Better," Trina said. "Thanks."

"Arty should be coming home soon. He's feeling so much better."

There was an awkward silence, then Arthur commented on how nice the house was.

"We've been here about six months now," Rosalie said. "Please have a seat. Can I get you something to drink?"

"No, thanks," the LaRues said at the same time.

Rosalie watched as Aunt Reba shook her head and went into the kitchen. Apparently, Trina saw her leave as well.

"Can I ask why you're here?" Trina said.

"We wanted to see how you're doing," her mother said.

"You could have called."

"Your number isn't listed," Arthur said.

"You could have gotten it from Aunt Reba."

There was more silence. Rosalie had heard a tinge of anger creep into Trina's voice.

"You can see I'm fine," Trina said. She stopped in frustration and said, "Rosalie. Please get them back in here."

"Trina," Rosalie said.

"Please."

Rosalie went into the kitchen and found Reba leaning against the sink and Juanito leaning against the refrigerator.

"Trina wants both of you in the living room."

"We're leaving," Reba said. She gave Rosalie a reassuring pat on the shoulder. "I'll be back in the morning to see about her."

When the three of them returned to the living room, Rosalie heard Trina say, "I want you to apologize to her. Both of you. It's gone on long enough."

There was another lengthy silence. Rosalie wasn't sure what happened while Trina was alone with them.

"Dad, you need to look at it this way," Trina said from the sofa. "Suppose you need a kidney some day. Aunt Reba might be the only one who'll be the perfect match for you." She sighed heavily. "Are you ready to take that chance? Life's too short. You need to get over it."

Mesmerized, Rosalie watched as Arthur LaRue nodded in agreement, and said, "That nice young man, Eric Vega told us that you and Reba were the only two in the family who went and had tests done besides your mother and me."

"Aunt Reba would also have given Arty a kidney," Trina said.

Rosalie was at a loss for words as she saw Trina's father sniff and nod again. He blinked away tears and then looked across the room at his sister, Reba.

"You've done more for my family than any of the others," he said. "Thank you for caring about both of my kids."

Reba nodded. "You're welcome."

"Rosalie," Trina said tiredly. "Write down our phone number and give it to them, please. I hate to be rude, but I need a pain pill."

"We were just leaving," Aunt Reba said. She came over to the sofa and kissed Trina on top of the head. "I'll be back in the morning to see about you." She hugged Rosalie and followed Juanito out the door.

"We'll be going too so you can get some rest," her mother said. "It's good seeing you again, Rosalie."

After walking them to the door, Rosalie knew she and Trina would be up for hours processing the day's events. She closed the door behind the LaRues and went over to the sofa. Kneeling down beside it, Rosalie looked at Trina and then kissed her on the lips.

"I can just see my father now," Trina said as their foreheads touched. "He'll be nice to Aunt Reba from now on just in case he ever needs a kidney. You watch."

Rosalie smiled. "Where did you get all this pessimism?"

Trina kissed her lightly on the nose. "You forget how well I know these people."

About the Author

Peggy J. Herring lives on seven acres of mesquite in south Texas with her cockatiel and green-eyed wooden cat. When she isn't writing, Peggy enjoys fishing, camping and traveling. She is the author of *Once More With Feeling, Love's Harvest, Hot Check, A Moment's Indiscretion, Those Who Wait* and *To Have and to Hold* from Naiad Press and *Calm Before the Storm* and *The Comfort of Strangers* from Bella Books. In addition, Peggy has contributed short stories to several Naiad anthologies, to include, *The First Time Ever, Dancing In the Dark, Lady Be Good, The Touch of Your Hand,* and *The Very Thought of You.* Peggy is currently working on a new romance titled *Distant Thunder* to be released by Bella Books in 2003.

Publications from
BELLA BOOKS, INC.
the best in contemporary lesbian fiction

P.O. Box 201007   Ferndale, MI 48220
Phone: 800-729-4992
www.bellabooks.com

RECOGNITION FACTOR by Claire McNab. 176 pp. Denise
Cleever tracks a notorious terrorist to America.
ISBN 1-931513-24-4 $12.95

NORA AND LIZ by Nancy Garden. 296 pp. Lesbian romance by
the author of "Annie on My Mind.   ISBN 1931513-20-1 $12.95

MIDAS TOUCH by Frankie J. Jones. 208 pp. Sandra had
everything but love.   ISBN 1-931513-21-X $12.95

BEYOND ALL REASON by Peggy J. Herring. 240 pp. A romance
hotter than Texas.   ISBN 1-9513-25-2 $12.95

ACCIDENTAL MURDER: 14th Detective Inspector Carol
Ashton Mystery by Claire McNab. 208 pp.Carol Ashton
tracks an elusive killer.   ISBN 1-931513-16-3 $12.95

SEEDS OF FIRE:Tunnel of Light Trilogy, Book 2 by Karin
Kallmaker writing as Laura Adams. 274 pp. Intriguing
sequel to *Sleight of Hand*.   ISBN 1-931513-19-8 $12.95

DRIFTING AT THE BOTTOM OF THE WORLD by
Auden Bailey. 288 pp. Beautifully written first novel set
in Antarctica.   ISBN 1-931513-17-1 $12.95

STREET RULES: A Detective Franco Mystery by
Baxter Clare. 304 pp. Gritty, fast-paced mystery with
compelling Detective L.A. Franco   ISBN 1-931513-14-7 $12.95

CLOUDS OF WAR by Diana Rivers. 288 pp. Women
unite to defend Zelindar!   ISBN 1-931513-12-0 $12.95

OUTSIDE THE FLOCK by Jackie Calhoun. 220 pp.
Searching for love, Jo finds temptation.   ISBN 1-931513-13-9 $12.95

WHEN GOOD GIRLS GO BAD: A Motor City Thriller by
Therese Szymanski. 230 pp. Brett, Randi, and Allie join
forces to stop a serial killer.   ISBN 1-931513-11-2 $12.95

DEATHS OF JOCASTA: The Second Micky Night Mystery
by J.M. Redmann. 408 pp. Sexy and intriguing Lambda
Literary Award nominated mystery.   ISBN 1-931513-10-4 $12.95

LOVE IN THE BALANCE by Marianne K. Martin. 256 pp.
The classic lesbian love story, back in print!
ISBN 1-931513-08-2 $12.95

EIGHTH DAY: A Cassidy James Mystery by Kate Calloway.
272 pp. In the eighth installment of the Cassidy James
mystery series, Cassidy goes undercover at a camp for
troubled teens.   ISBN 1-931513-04-X $11.95

MIRRORS by Marianne K. Martin. 208 pp. Jean Carson and
Shayna Bradley fight for a future together.
                                                   ISBN 1-931513-02-3 $11.95

THE ULTIMATE EXIT STRATEGY: A Virginia Kelly
Mystery by Nikki Baker. 240 pp. The long-awaited return of
the wickedly observant Virginia Kelly.   ISBN 1-931513-03-1 $11.95

FOREVER AND THE NIGHT by Laura DeHart Young.
224 pp. Desire and passion ignite the frozen Arctic in this
exciting sequel to the classic romantic adventure *Love on
the Line*.   ISBN 0-931513-00-7 $11.95

WINGED ISIS by Jean Stewart. 240 pp. The long-awaited
sequel to *Warriors of Isis* and the fourth in the exciting
Isis series.   ISBN 1-931513-01-5 $11.95

ROOM FOR LOVE by Frankie J. Jones. 192 pp. Jo and
Beth must overcome the past in order to have a future
together.   ISBN 0-9677753-9-6 $11.95

THE QUESTION OF SABOTAGE by Bonnie J. Morris.
144 pp. A charming, sexy tale of romance, intrigue, and
coming of age.   ISBN 0-9677753-8-8 $11.95

SLEIGHT OF HAND by Karin Kallmaker writing as
Laura Adams. 256 pp. A journey of passion, heartbreak
and triumph that reunites two women for a final chance
at their destiny.   ISBN 0-9677753-7-X $11.95

MOVING TARGETS: A Helen Black Mystery by Pat Welch.
240 pp. Helen must decide if getting to the bottom of a
mystery is worth hitting bottom.   ISBN 0-9677753-6-1 $11.95

CALM BEFORE THE STORM by Peggy J. Herring. 208
pp. Colonel Robicheaux retires from the military and
comes out of the closet.   ISBN 0-9677753-1-0 $12.95

OFF SEASON by Jackie Calhoun. 208 pp. Pam threatens
Jenny and Rita's fledgling relationship.   ISBN 0-9677753-0-2 $11.95

WHEN EVIL CHANGES FACE: A Motor City Thriller
by Therese Szymanski. 240 pp. Brett Higgins is back in
another heart-pounding thriller.   ISBN 0-9677753-3-7 $11.95

BOLD COAST LOVE by Diana Tremain Braund. 208 pp.
Jackie Claymont fights for her reputation and the right to
love the woman she chooses.   ISBN 0-9677753-2-9 $11.95

THE WILD ONE by Lyn Denison. 176 pp. Rachel never
expected that Quinn's wild yearnings would change her
life forever.   ISBN 0-9677753-4-5 $12.95

**Visit
Bella Books
at
www.bellabooks.com**